Times to Try the Soul of Man

Kenneth Weene

Times to Try the Soul of Man

Copyright © 2015 by Kenneth Weene

ISBN 13: 9780990715870

Library of Congress Control Number: 2015936188

Cover design by All Things That Matter Press
Published in 2015 by All Things That Matter Press

For
Armando
whose death in 1999 inspired this
work of fiction.

Thanks
to the people whose lives
included the real events which underlie this tale –
those in New York, South America, and yes, those from Israel.

With sorrow for those who perished
9/11/2001.

Personal appreciation to D.P. who introduced me to many of the facts
from which this tale has been created.

Great respect to those elected and appointed officials who do their jobs
without expectation of personal gain.

Works of fiction hold the deepest truths for they explore the human
spirit and celebrate the growth of the individual soul. While based on
actual events, this is a work of fiction. Any resemblance of its
characters to persons living or dead is entirely coincidental.

Prologue: The Wakeup Call

If the sex had been better, I wouldn't have noticed the shaking of my bed. Marcie and I had been living together for three months, two months too long. The quality of our sex had already become a casualty.

We shared my one-room, walk-up hovel on the fourth floor of a decrepit Lower Eastside dumpsite which the landlord's ad called "well located" and "charming." The location, right in the middle of what New Yorkers call Alphabet City, was convenient, as long as the tenant didn't need to get to the subways or anywhere else. The charm, well, that was a figment of the landlord's imagination, just as the love between us was a figment of Marcie's.

At least I had a place of my own: no more living with my father, sharing a dorm room, or living in a pensione like the one in Santiago where I had spent the past year studying Spanish and traveling around South America. That's where I met Marcie, Mo, and Estrella. Estrella, green-eyed Estrella, I wish ….

I came back to the States, back to the Big Apple and to the approaching new millennium, and looked forward to new women. There followed hundreds of emails and phone calls, that must have set Marcie's old man back a bundle, during which she asked, no, begged to come to New York. "*No puedo vivir sin tu*. I can't live without you," she crooned in lilting Spanish and accented English.

I gave in. I wasn't sure I could live with her, but sometimes the balls take over and the brain gets decommissioned.

Marcie came. I met her at Kennedy and drove my dilapidated Datsun straight back to my place. We fucked before she unpacked. That sex had been good, better than good. In fact, sex the first couple of weeks had been great, maybe even spectacular. The next two or three weeks had been all right. By the third month the music stopped, the dance was over, and still she hung on. After only three months of playing house, I could understand why my old man had been so willing to give up on my mother when she took off with Paul.

That morning, eleven o'clock, whatever my cock was doing, my heart was not really into it. Better than jerking off? Sure. Better than a peep show? Maybe. Better than finding someone else? No way.

Marcie had no clue on top, practically jumping up and down in excitement, moaning in Spanish. For a girl raised in middle-class Chilean society and educated in Catholic schools, she sure was ready to screw.

Whoever said, "Repression breeds desire" certainly knew about Marcie.

My head was miles away. For one thing, I was depressed as hell. Not just about Marcie, but everything. Out of money. My car, which barely ran, had been towed once again. I hadn't been to any of my classes in weeks. My job as a reporter at a weekly newspaper in East Elmhurst, the far end of Queens, paid crap. My mother was back in the nut factory—third time since she walked out, each time after another relationship that was going to be "wonderful" and ended in tears. And, just to add the cherry to the sundae, I was about out of friends. All of which I could have tolerated if the sex had still been good. Suddenly, the bed shook left and right, front and back, like some kind of Coney Island fun-ride. The motion gave me something to focus on.

In terror-driven slow motion, I watched cockroaches scurry in purposeless circles on the brown-tinged walls. *What the hell. When the roaches are frightened, you know you have trouble.*

I must have said something. Marcie paused her pumping and asked if she had hurt me. Before I could think of an answer, the whole building twitched.

"Get off," I bellowed. "I think the fucking building is coming down. Grab your clothes and come on."

By the time Marcie pulled the apartment door closed I was halfway down the stairs, buttoning my shirt, and thanking God that there weren't many other people still in the building. By eleven, most of the tenants had dispersed to jobs and school. All except for Jack, who drove a nightshift cab and who, just ahead of me, was charging toward the narrow front door onto Avenue B.

Once outside and standing on the cracked and pitted sidewalk, I watched people streaming north toward the corner of Fourth Street.

There they turned east and headed for the river. I caught my breath while Marcie caught up with me. Pulling her by the arm, I followed the crowd. Two thoughts clanged in my head: *When did I become a lemming? Is there a story here?*

We struggled to keep up with the surging crowd. Periodic booms came from the direction towards which we were all streaming. Not the sharp report of a gun, it was more a deep-throated growling thunder, a sound like an old cannon. Boom … Boom … Boom.

We rounded the corner onto Avenue C along with hundreds of other people who materialized from stores and apartments, adding to the surging flow on sidewalks. Marcie held my hand and trailed behind. I felt the pull of her slowness on my shoulder.

"Hurry." I tugged forward.

Just north of the intersection was a community garden, one of the small vacant lot gardens the city had been trying to close down. Beautiful mixtures of flowers and produce and decorated with found art, these bits of artificially created country added charm to the Lower East Side, but they did shit for the all-important tax base. City Hall was not interested in aesthetics, especially not in the low-rent district.

There was an enormous gap where the garden's fence had been replaced by loose hanging chain-link held closed in place by lengths of wire. Inside the garden stood a crane, complete with wrecking ball, and a dump truck. Both had engines running; both were decorated with a jagged mountain logo and the name Mannlich Construction in dark red letters.

The heavy steel ball bashed into a shattered building which the night before had been the homes of students, couples, families. Each whack of ball produced one of those echoing, shuddering booms.

People, now suddenly dispossessed, homeless and helpless, gathered on the sidewalk, moaning and grumbling in a polyglot of languages and accents.

"They gave us less than an hour's notice," a black woman holding the hand of a terrified toddler told no one in particular.

"They were banging on the doors and yelling the building was coming down. I grabbed … where …?" The dazed elderly man sat rocking on the curb. He clutched his possessions wrapped in an old blanket, rocked back and forth, and cried. Next to him stood a small, framed, yellowed photograph of a young woman. The glass was cracked. "Delores," he sobbed as he picked it up. "Oh, oh, ohhh."

Two police officers, the first a young man who, disturbed by the events around him, fidgeted and vigilantly tried to look in every direction at once. The second, a somewhat older woman, struck a nonchalant pose as if she could care less.

The two cops stood on the sidewalk between the hapless survivors and the boss of the demolition team. He wore a cheap suit of polyester blue—bagged around his knees and shoulders—and held a bullhorn in his right hand. Through it, he tried to tell the workmen what to do. They ignored him with studied indifference. New York workers, safe in union seniority, knowing just how unimportant their boss was.

The garden had been uprooted. Two men wielding sledgehammers and pry bars were breaking whatever remained of the urban salvage which had been used to decorate it, into bits. In one corner of the lot the workers had piled plastic garbage bags filled with plants, which had as recently as that morning been carefully tended. One, lone, defiant tomato vine and its stake had somehow been overlooked.

Damn, wish I had my camera. Great pic. Front page stuff. Good story. Sell it to the Village News.

The crowd grew restive and ugly. The policewoman called for backup. I wondered if that wouldn't make things worse. Perhaps make a better story. Again, I wished I had taken my camera. I considered running back to the apartment and braving its uncertain footing. I might have, but Marcie clung to me with the terror and strength of the drowning.

Clouds of dust emanated from each stroke of the giant ball. Some workmen wore respirators, others had bandanas over their mouths and noses. The crowd hacked and coughed. Gray dust settled everywhere. Faces took on a ghoulish appearance as angry and frightened eyes peered out from ash-gray skin.

A good story was breaking and the possibility it would get even better was heralded by the whine of more police cars.

Then a new sound, singing in Spanish, a song about comrades willing to face death for the sake of the cause, the cause of freedom, the cause of justice.

The sound welled as the singers rounded the corner. They numbered in the thirties, but the energy of their voices made them a throng. A short, middle-aged man led them. Dressed in jeans, a flannel shirt, and work boots, clean-shaven except for a small mustache. He wore raccoon glasses ringing his eyes in thick black frames. I had never seen him in the neighborhood, but the reaction of the crowd was loud and welcoming. Men reached to take his hand or slap his shoulders. Women pointed him out to their children.

The crowd parted as he approached; people fell into line behind him and added their voices to the song.

This was my introduction to Jose Figurés, president of the Lower East Side Latino Community Center, a man whose life and death were to change me.

Figurés stood opposite the man with the bullhorn. The singing stopped. Conversation stopped. The crane's motor stopped. The dump truck's motor stopped. The workers stood still. The two original police officers, now joined by half-a-dozen of their peers, surrounded the two men.

Silence.

When collective nerves were ready to break, Figurés spoke, first in Spanish and then again in English. He demanded the work be stopped.

"This is a community garden that you have desecrated. We are the community." He waved his left arm to include all of us standing there watching.

The crowd bellowed its support, "*¡Somos la comunidad!*" and pushed inward toward the confrontation.

"We want you to leave."

"*¡Váyanse! ¡Quéramos que usted vayan!*" the crowd echoed.

The man with the bullhorn, his voice distorted by static, tried to respond. I caught something about city permits and work orders through the hail of catcalls, jeers, and the growing chant, "*¡Somos la comunidad! ¡Somos la comunidad!*"

While Figurés spoke, the workers became increasingly uneasy: shifting their weight from foot-to-foot, stepping back, and finally standing with their backs to the heavy equipment. A few of them whispered to one another; some picked up tools and lengths of rebar. It was one thing for them to ignore their boss, it was another for the angry mob to show so little respect for the authority he represented and under which they worked.

The project director turned his frustration and his bullhorn on the police. "Do something. We have permits. Get them out of here." The amplified, crackling, tinny words elicited a roar of anger and more chanting from the crowd.

I screamed along with my neighbors. As the mob moved and shifted, those neighbors alternately spoke English, Spanish, and sometimes other languages.

My own voice yelling in Spanish and then in English — my choice of language dictated by the language closest to my ears. What I yelled, I can't remember; I just know I yelled along with hundreds of others. In the moment of emotion we became one. A mob had been birthed.

The police looked around and shook their heads; heroism did not require them to be fools. The original young male cop fingered his gun. His partner reached over and pulled his hand away.

The job manager again demanded action. A newly arrived sergeant, now apparently the ranking police officer, put his hand on the man's wrist and held it so that he could no longer use the bullhorn.

The sergeant spoke with great animation, first to the manager and then to Figurés. I could not hear what was said, but it was clear the sergeant had no intention of taking on the growing crowd. It was also clear from the way they squared off that there was no love lost between him and Figurés. But, there was respect, respect which the sergeant didn't show to the project manager.

The three men yammered for a few minutes. I wondered how they could concentrate. The tension of the moment became palpable in the mumbling discontent of the crowd. Occasional catcalls of derision and anger followed by shouted approvals in English and Spanish punctuated the air.

At last, the manager gestured for the workers to open the makeshift gate. They followed his instructions, keeping weapons in-hand, backs to the equipment, and a wary eye on the ever-growing, motley crowd.

If the mob charged into the garden, the workers would be overwhelmed and the police would have to take action. The situation verged on riot.

Marcie, terrified, was pulling me away. I held her hand but didn't budge.

Some of the people closest to the fence moved forward. Figurés stepped into the center of the opening, faced the crowd, and held his hands in the air. Everyone stopped. The pushing stopped. The talking stopped. Alphabet City held her breath.

Figurés, now in control, waited until the silence was complete. He spoke first in Spanish and then again in English. "We have won a minor skirmish. The workers are leaving. Let them go in peace. Tomorrow a judge will decide if they have the right to tear down this building. For today, we have won. *Hemos Ganado, por hoy.*"

I looked at Figurés's face and saw a great weariness. I also saw the iron resolve of a leader, of a shepherd who would never desert his flock. At that moment, although I had not actually met him, I truly liked the man, liked and respected him.

"There are people, our friends, our neighbors, who have lost their homes today," Figurés continued. "We must help them. We must save our community. Please, bring whatever you can to the community center."

Figurés turned to the dispossessed. "We will create a shelter for you and help you find a new place. We will not abandon you. *No le abandonaremos.*"

The dispossessed cheered. We all cheered. Even a couple of the workers cheered. It was clear that this was a man who commanded authority, the voice of the people with a soft New York, Puerto Rican accent. *"No lo' abandonaremo'."*

Gently, Figurés reached down to the old man, who, silent and still rocking, clutched his precious photograph to his breast.

"Ven, amigo mío," Figurés almost whispered. He helped the old man to his feet, and shouldered the blanket holding the man's meager ration

of salvaged possession. *"Ven, amigo mío,"* he repeated. They walked arm-in-arm, slowly, at the old man's pace.

Much of the crowd followed.

Sometimes a good story just comes up and bites a reporter in the ass. I resolved to learn more about this leader, to interview him, to write about him, and to write about this new urban warfare: an urban warfare that had literally shaken me out of bed.

This may win me a Pulitzer.

A community in turmoil, a building full of newly homeless, a group of terrified workers, nervous cops, and a charismatic stranger who seemed to truly care, yeah, it was a story. And me, I was thinking about getting a prize.

I took Marcie's arm and pulled her through the crowd and back toward my apartment.

"Let's get a coffee," she suggested as we passed a café, "or, perhaps go home, back to our bed. *Podríamos hacer el amor.*" There was bait in her voice.

"Let's not," I responded. "I've got to get to the paper."

Yeah, there was a story to write. Whatever else, I was going to get my story. I didn't know it then, but what a story it was going to be, a story of crime and terror and of that one terrible day when the towers fell.

Chapter 1: Learning

A loner, never one to be part of a group, the only activity I ever willingly joined was the high school newspaper. I wrote a couple of stories that documented some of the less seemly sides of Cantigua High and earned me an interview with an uncomfortable principal. Mr. Sacks had not liked the first article discussing drug sales on campus. He'd been even more upset when my next piece put teachers in the middle of some of those transactions.

"Who told you this stuff?" he demanded.

I shrugged my shoulders.

"I'll call your father in." His scowl no doubt intended to scare me.

"Freedom of the press." I sneered. I knew as upset as Sacks might be, this peapod of a man would be terrified by the thought of court cases. "You know the A.C.L.U. has—"

"Nicholas, you have some real problems." The principal used his grownup authority voice, stopping a beat between each of the carefully enunciated word, which added to my merriment. "I think you need to figure out what your goals are. Just what do you want to get out of your education? What do you want to do with your life?" He cleared his throat and picked at one of the spots of egg that dotted his blue and red striped tie.

Having made notes in what he assured me was my permanent record, a document that would, he insisted, affect the rest of my life, Sacks dismissed me.

The next day I received another summons. This one from Mrs. Kantor, the guidance counselor, a want-to-be shrink. Every school, at least every school on Long Island, has a Mrs. Evelyn Kantor, an armful short of a bushel, and too many half-understood psych books for anybody's good.

It had been decided and agreed to by my old man that I would spend three hours a week with this font of mis-wisdom.

Since Mrs. Kantor fancied herself a Freudian, she asked about my mother, our relationship, and why she had left home. I talked about Paul and the houseboat in Key West on which they were going to live before he became the first of the progression of her failed romances. I left out the marijuana and the cocaine and my dad's supposed affairs; no sense giving the guidance counselor any bones to worry at.

Kantor did ask about my father and about the women who came and just as easily went in his life, women whom more often than not I met over breakfast only to have them never reappear. I said, "He's cool," and left her there.

The guidance counselor ascribed my interest in journalism to latent voyeurism.

"You like to watch," she insisted while smirking in that knowing way adults use. It meant, "Don't try to tell me anything. I'm already right."

I took the unintended bait and submitted an editorial about the need for the school to look more realistically at student sex, including the seven abortions I knew about, seven in that half school year. Within the week I was off the paper. The faculty advisor said I wasn't suited for journalism. I told her she was a toad.

The newspaper had been the most fun I had in school except for maybe the hours I spent getting high. By graduation I'd decided on a career in journalism.

Dad suggested taking classes part-time at Pace. "It's in the city. Not too far from the garage. We can commute together."

It was a decent idea; no newspaper would have hired me just out of high school. The days of "Hey, copyboy" and hawking papers on the streets were long gone. A few college classes would at least give me the appearance of doing something worthwhile. I signed up for three courses and got a dead-end job in a record store, the kind of work a monkey could do.

I did decently in those college classes, surprisingly well considering my high school grades. Mostly, that was due to commuting into Manhattan with Dad. I got to school because he was with me right to the front of the campus. Once there, there wasn't much else to do, so I went to class and studied. By then, I'd figured out that marijuana and I were not a winning team. Those lousy grades in high school and the fenders of Dad's car could tell the story.

The record store was only a couple of blocks from Pace. One great benefit: they gave employee discounts. Even better, I got some good chitchat with primo snatch. Amazing how many young women come into a record store. More amazing how many are eager to talk with a total stranger if he's wearing an employee I.D.

It was in the store I met my first Latina, Deidre, a Dominican with a pretty face, big boobs, and an ass in constant motion. Deidre was a regular. She came in every day about one o'clock and bopped around to the music. We all knew she was boosting CDs, but the managers said leave her alone because the customers got really turned on by her shimmying and shaking and they ended up buying. Letting her steal was way cheaper than paying her to shill.

I made it with Deidre even though she pretended she couldn't speak English. We made it pretty regularly for a couple of months. At the end, I had crabs, gonorrhea, and a love for everything Latin, especially women. The first two took me to an urologist by the name of Itsch, whom I, and the other sleazes I met in his waiting room, nicknamed Itchy Balls. The last inspired my curiosity about South America and my interest in learning Spanish.

Dad, delighted with what seemed like my new academic motivation, agreed to foot the bill. I was off for a year abroad—my year in Chile.

Chapter 2: Santiago

If I had expected Chile to be a new experience, I would have been disappointed. Nothing against the country, its people, or their culture; I had brought myself along, and that guy was just not ready for different.

Right off, I resented the other people living in the pensione. Most of them were from Europe, already spoke passable Spanish, and looked down on Americans as uncivilized louts. I didn't disappoint them. I had never been a wine drinker, but I learned my way to all the nearby wine bars and how to order a glass along with a ham sandwich. At least it was in Spanish.

I spent my first couple of weeks in Santiago living on *sandwich jamón* and drinking cheap *vino tinto*. When sufficiently drunk, I migrated to a café to enjoy the sobering effects of máte as hot and as sweet as I could get.

My favorite café was Rodolfo's on *Avenida de los Mártires*: a dark place where the music incessantly punched at my guts while the whine and blinking light of video games made my head ache. The thing I loved about the place was the girls who made it home base, all of them students showing their independence and uniqueness by hanging out in a group and discussing social science, philosophy, and the evils of the United State.

Who are they trying to impress?

Deep down a different story played in my head. They were sexy; I was horny. Damn, I wanted them. I kept coming back.

Try as I might, I never really understood enough of their arguments to take part, but I did learn some Spanish, which made up for the classes I was skipping. Without Dad's riding herd on me, I had slipped right back to my high school ways. Take pot out and put wine and máte in and you have good old me—a basic bum. If Estrella had not taken a shine to me, that would have been the end of things. But she took me on as her personal project.

Estrella was a good kid. She made up for her lack of looks with a caring heart and an instant laugh. Not one of the university girls, she was a waitress. Some of the college kids, the stuck-up bitchy ones, made sure she remembered her role. Calling her *camarera* or even *chica*, they would laugh as they dropped their change into the dregs of their máte, a tip with a message. That didn't bother Estrella. She laughed good-naturedly at their jibes and ignored the temptation to spit in their drinks before she served them. Perhaps, had she heard their crueler comments about her appearance, she would have been more tempted.

Estrella was heavy-set, her buttocks large and droopy. When she was out of hearing range, the nastier patrons would refer to her as *bigote* in cruel reference to the hairiness of her upper lip. Nobody mentioned the one aspect of her appearance that captivated me: her sweet, shining, light-lime colored eyes. Unique, they gave outward appearance to her gentle character. When she turned them on me, my ubiquitous anger would cool for the moment and I would allow a quick smile to supplant my habitual scowl.

For me, Estrella was a caretaker. An instinctive mother, she slipped me extra food when her boss wasn't looking and then insist I eat it.

"*Es bueno para el salud,*" she would say each time she brought another unordered plate.

When business was slow, Estrella sat with me and patiently taught me basic Spanish. Her greatest flaw, a concern about my drinking: "*Usted siempre viene a bebe aquí.*"

I enjoyed her company enough to sometimes, not often, but occasionally, come in for a máte without a trip to the wine bar first.

I don't know if Estrella wanted to sleep with me. I do know that I wanted to sleep with her—not from physical attraction, but with the horniness that comes from weeks without combined with an adolescent fantasy of the pureness and redemptive nature of sex. Which one of us it would redeem, I had no idea.

With unthinking juvenile fervor I simply wanted to get laid. If I were unable to make an entrée with the college crowd, I could at least satisfy myself with something less. Sex is a selfish goddess.

In bumbling Spanish rehearsed with dictionary in hand, I made my approach. "*¿Usted tiene sexo con mí?*"

To my joyful amazement Estrella said *si* in the same soft, caring, motherly voice she used when she asked if I wanted another máte , suggested I drink less wine, or told me to forget the check.

I don't think Estrella would have denied me anything, but she did insist we make love as part of a date, not just a quick trip to her bedroom.

That was reasonable enough. I took her to a movie, an action American flick with Spanish subtitles. I spent most of the movie with my hungry lips buried in Estrella's neck and ear with an occasional foray to her lips. She would gently push me away so she could watch the film.

After the movie, I wanted to go to her apartment for some action, but Estrella had other plans. As best I could understand, her roommate wouldn't be going out for another hour. We spent that hour in a coffee shop.

It was a snazzy place, much more ambiance than Rodolfo's, heavier prices, too. Same kind of clientele, but with better clothes. Estrella ordered a sandwich and máte for us both.

We drank the máte through a metal straw, which we passed back and forth. It was no big deal, not a major cross-cultural experience, but I was happy to finally be sharing something with someone.

Just when we started to slurp the second *guampa*, Marcie walked in.

It was lust at first sight. Svelte, well dressed, with auburn hair, deep dark eyes accented with skillful makeup, and a figure from the fashion magazines, Marcie was something out of my fantasies. At that moment, with one bird already in hand, I felt sure enough of myself to try for the one in the bush. Sex isn't just selfish, she's also a narcissistic goddess.

Poor Estrella, I gave her no thought, not even an, "Excuse me," as I levitated from the table and floated on a sea of desire and testosterone to greet this totally desirable stranger.

I stumbled through a greeting. *"No pienso que hemos satisfecho,"* and stuck out my hand.

She laughed.

A mistake? Damn!

I reddened.

One of the men seated near the door laughed and called me a *Yanqui.* He tried to make it sound friendly and funny. Maybe he even meant it that way. I figured he didn't want me messing with *his* Chilean goddess. Testosterone pumping, I was ready to go at him.

Besides, a little macho might impress her.

Marcie read the situation and took my arm, turning me away from the table of guys. "What's your name?" she asked with accented English in a voice that made my cavities sit up and take notice.

I answered and asked hers.

"Marcie, Marcella Consuela Garcia Desséo."

"That's a lot of name."

"*No hay problema,* you can call me Marcie. Do you want to share some máte?"

Are you kidding?

I was more than wanting.

I let Marcie steer me to a table right near Estrella, who, head hanging, looked ready to cry.

I looked again, and she was crying.

I gestured for the waitress and slipped her money to pay for Estrella. I'm sure that waitress thought I was a bastard. I'd agree, but that's how things go when a guy is young, dumb, and in rut.

The waitress whispered in Estrella's ear. She stood, shaking, and let the waitress help her to the door. I guess she was used to getting dumped by pigs like me. I'd have to find another place for my máte drinking, but that didn't seem like a big sacrifice—not if it meant sitting there with Marcella Consuela Garcia Desséo.

For whatever reason, Marcie liked me, but sleeping together was going to be another story. It was definitely going to take more than a date.

Marcie came from a good, upper-middle-class, Catholic upbringing. Her parents had reluctantly allowed her to go to the university, their major reason: the desirability of an educated son-in-law. During her first year at college they insisted she come home right after classes. Dates were to be supervised by her younger brother, who loved lording it over her.

Now, in her second year, Marcie insisted on more autonomy; her parents, again reluctantly, acquiesced. In Marcie's world, autonomy had not meant sex, drugs, or even rock-and-roll. An occasional evening spent in a coffee house talking with one of the young men she'd met at school and who seemed like appropriate matches would suffice.

Possibly, probably, if her "date" of that evening had been at the café when she arrived, Marcie would have ignored me, and I would have lusted from afar. I would have gone home with Estrella, maybe to find out that she was an incredible lay, maybe to find out that she was an incredible love, maybe to fall in love for the rest of my life. At least I've always imagined that, especially when thinking back on how trying and boring the relationship with Marcie eventually became.

As it was, I counted myself lucky when Jorge, Marcie's scheduled date, did show up twenty minutes after she and I had ordered our first máte. By then, we were already busily talking and laughing in a mixture or languages. Jorge said something hurriedly in Spanish, something I didn't understand, but the tone of which was unmistakably angry, and walked out.

Marcie's response, "¡Ni que fuera tuya!" echoed as the door slammed behind him.

Shit, this is cool.

"Let a Chilean boy *toqcar mis pechos* and he thinks he owns me. *¡Qué se vaya a la mierda!*"

I kissed her dark red lips and pulled her body tight against mine.

She stiffened and then relaxed in my hold.

So fucking cool.

Wine bars, cafes, movies, walks; we dated, held hands, kissed, and touched, all at Marcie's pace.

She was wonderfully serious about our relationship. Marcie was a virgin and remained one for the first month, one week, and three days of our relationship, during which period I met her parents, her brothers, her sister, and, it seemed, everyone else of importance in her family.

Her father, a respected lawyer, grilled me on my family. He was placated when I told him my father planned a visit over Easter. I didn't tell him that Dad's current live-in girlfriend might come along, if they stayed together long enough, which was unlikely.

When Marcie finally agreed to have sex, I almost felt guilty. *"Te amo tanto,"* she crooned and licked her lips seductively.

"Yeah, me, too." I choked the words out.

Marcie had traversed a mental divide across which she could never return. I knew that she, at least at some level, had resolved that we should marry: an idea as foreign to me as the customs and language by which I was surrounded. I'd watched my parents' marriage dissolve in bickering, paranoia, and infidelity. I'd watched my mother's mind dissolve in a sequence of *forever* relationships. In my mind marriage was not an option, and I doubted it ever would be. Marcie was a trophy; she was gorgeous and she was Latin, but she was not my life.

After a hesitant start, Marcie became sex-starved. Sex can be an insatiable god. At once submissive and demanding, she satisfied my every whim and desire and then demanded more. Many nights my libido and my capacity were exhausted long before her hunger had been sated. At least she settled for my tongue and fingers.

For all the action and the exhaustion, I wanted other women; Marcie was not enough.

Would any woman ever be?

Diversity was my instinct. Experimentation called at every corner. The more emotionally and physically attached Marcie became, the more eager I became to meet other women. It didn't help that Santiago was filled with dusky women with big breasts and tight, swaying asses.

It was more to get away from the oppressive heat of our relationship than any intellectual interest that motivated me to ask Dad for money to travel around the continent. I explained that I would travel by the least expensive means and stay at hostels.

"That way I'll be forced to speak Spanish, not like at school where most of the kids want to practice their English." The lie even sounded good to me.

He put some cash in my account, and I was ready for my next experience.

Chapter 3: The Sons of Israel

Machu Picchu, the mystical Incan city, is said to hold the sun in its ambit. High in the mountains of Peru, it was one of the wonders of the pre-Columbian world. Today, in our world of scientific marvels, its beauty continues to draw tourists.

Dad agreed there were two places in South America I should see: Easter Island, a trip he would take with me at Easter and the other Machu Picchu. It's high above sea level, and he feared he wouldn't be able to hike and climb once he got there. That's why he wanted me to go and bring back photographs and tell him all about it. For that purpose, and probably to let me know that I was still loved even if I was a bum, he sent me a new camera, the one I still use, an SLR from Japan, a journal, and traveling money.

The first leg of the journey was easy; board a plane in Santiago and get off in Lima. Once in Jorge Chavez airport, things took a downward turn.

The Peruvian authorities checked me out, a scruffy American, college age kid, and promptly ransacked my backpack and sleeping bag.

One of them looked in my wallet, where I had my return ticket and enough Chilean money cover the trip, be it at minimal standards. Demanding I take off my boots and socks, he grunted disappointment when there was no money hidden. He and another guard pulled out my camera and snapped a couple pictures of themselves so I wouldn't forget them. No doubt disappointed that I hadn't lived down to their expectations that a gringo college kid should be carrying drugs and extra money for which I would be forced to enrich them with a bribe, they passed me on my way. I found a restroom and checked that my extra money and ATM card were still securely fastened to my side with adhesive tape. I'd learned that trick from Miguel, one of the friendlier guys at the pensione.

A visitor from Portugal, Miguel had learned it the hard way from a customs agent in Uruguay, and years later I bet he still nurses the damp weather pain of cracked ribs that accompanied the lesson.

"Whatever you do," Miguel insisted, "don't put anything into your socks. That's the first place they look. '*Quí tate los zapatos.*' That's the first thing they'll say to you."

Are your serious? Whoa, exactly where I planned to hide—oh, shit!

Thanks to Miguel I made it through Peruvian customs without anything more than a little taunting and a couple of photographs I later used as dart boards until they became too ripped to bother.

I took the airport bus to downtown Lima. I had the address of a hostel provided by my "Study Spanish Abroad" program. I had little faith or interest in the program, but figured the *Mesón Para los Estudiantes del Mundo* would be as good a place to flop as any. I told the driver the address. He nodded and said, "*Sí, sí, señor. Ningún problema.*"

The hostel was just a couple of blocks from the bus stop. The cabby, true to his trade, drove me around for ten minutes running up the meter and all the while telling me he knew a better place. I was not getting a real positive attitude about Peru.

The hostel didn't help. It looked like even the fleas had given up. The front room, which served as reception, lounge, and breakfast room, didn't have a single decent piece of furniture. What cushions there were had long since been ripped and badly mended with raggedly torn swatches of tape. The couch sagged and humped in so many places that it resembled a miniature mountain range. Scores of previous travelers had etched their names into tabletops, walls, and chairs. I immediately nicknamed the place "The Tattooed Whore," *La Puta Tatuada*. At least my Spanish was improving.

Management took the form of a squeaky-voiced pimple face. He gave me a bed assignment in one of the men's dorms, sheets, a thin blanket, a ragged towel, and a list of rules. The rules, in five languages, started out with an admonition: DO NOT DEFACE THE PROPERTY.

I crumpled the papers into my pocket.

There were six beds in the dorm, five of them occupied by a group who spoke a language that seemed vaguely familiar but was certainly not related to Spanish or English. One of the men said something, and they all laughed. A part of me burned, figuring they were talking about me.

"Spanish or English?" one of the men asked in heavily accented Spanish.

"What?"

"Would you prefer we speak Spanish or English?"

"English, my Spanish sucks."

"English it is. My name's Morris; my friends call me Mo." A handsome, dark-complexioned man about thirty with already thinning hair, Mo gave the immediate sense of self-assurance. The strength of his grip drove that sense home.

His accented English registered. I didn't have many friends as a kid, but I still managed to be invited to a couple of Bar Mitzvahs. "You guys Israeli?"

Mo nodded, grinned, and said, "I thought you'd figure we were Aussies."

Another fellow shot out his hand. "We were wondering how long it would take you to figure it out. I hope you don't mind spending the night with a bunch of Jews."

"Not if you can live with a fallen Episcopalian."

An appreciative chuckle.

"You aren't going to circumcise me in my sleep?"

"Only if you snore."

More laughter.

My new friends introduced themselves. Abe, Matt, and David appeared to be as affable as Mo. The fifth member of their group, Bernie, a bit older than the others, somewhat more serious and distant. While Mo encouraged me to have dinner with them, Bernie watched my face carefully. He was evaluating every nuance that might show itself. Watching him watch me, I noticed that Mo and the others were also watching Bernie's reactions.

A leader or just a judge? Whatever.

Abe spelled out the restrictions on their choices of meals and how far they were willing to compromise their religious strictures. Who cared? Israelis or not. Jews or not. Kosher or not. The simple reality, I would have gladly eaten sawdust in order to have the company of some friendly, English speaking guys.

With the slightest nod of his head, Bernie made it clear that I'd be welcomed.

"It's settled then," said Mo. "We'll go to the vegetarian restaurant."

"Sounds good to me." My mouth immediately watered for pork chops.

They surrounded me, patted my shoulders, gave me a couple of hugs. Even Bernie put his hand on my arm as we started down the street.

Lots of times a guy just falls in with bad companions, but this was an anomaly, I had fallen into good company. I'd never been to a summer sleep-away camp, now I was in the middle of a group of happy campers.

Over supper my new Israeli friends talked about their upcoming trip to Machu Picchu. "Hey, Nick, why don't you join us?" Mo suggested.

"Yeah, man, we have two jeeps, more than enough room for six of us," David added.

"I have no camping gear, sleeping bag, none of that shit," I protested.

"We have extra," Bernie said, "you're welcome to use it."

"It'll be great," Abe added. "The City of the Sun; the Incas used to worship the sun up there."

"Well, I … I'm not sure." I hemmed and hawed.

No way I can afford this. Jeeps, fancy equipment. I better take the train.

"The jeeps and everything are all paid for. Think of the money you'll be saving," Bernie said.

My hesitation dissolved. I was immediately thinking of the fun I could have with Dad's money. "I should chip in something."

"Yeah, yeah, sure. Don't worry about it. Maybe you'll treat to an ice cream." Mo clapped me on the shoulders. "It's going to be fun."

The next morning Bernie asked if I'd go with Matt and pick up some last-minute food. "We'll get the jeeps loaded. Just make sure your bag is ready before you head out."

Matt and I picked up eggs and cheese, some bread, cookies, cans of fruit, nothing that required a lot of thinking. I was chomping at the bit, but Matt was taking his time.

"Don't you want to get back?"

"The mountains won't move," he answered. "They've been patient for a long time."

We were already in the checkout line. Suddenly, Matt decided, "I think maybe we need some olive oil."

Another delay while he compared more labels.

By the time Matt and I got back to the hostel, the jeeps were piled high. Abe stood next to one last large box. It looked like a footlocker, but sturdier.

"Want a hand?" I offered.

Abe looked over at Bernie, who nodded.

"Yeah, sure. Grab an end."

I pulled on one of the handles. "Jesus, this is heavy. What have you got in it?" I strained at the weight.

"Just gear," Mo responded. "We don't want any surprises, last minute shortages."

That monster on board, we were ready, making our way through the mid-morning traffic. Mo, who sat behind me in the second jeep, tried to teach me an Israeli song.

Meatballs, maybe Ferris Bueller's Day Off? It's like I'm in the middle of one hell of a movie.

By lunchtime we'd reached bouncing, jouncing roads and miniature traffic jams caused by slow-paced pack animals and occasionally even slower buses.

We stopped around four, having found a campsite. It was an amazing spot. I couldn't figure out how we found it. Suddenly, the first jeep, driven by Abe, shot left off the road and up a bumpy, vine-encased track. Another sudden turn on an even more difficult path brought us to this small clearing surrounded with gorgeous, fragrant flowers. Abe and Matt, who had been driving our jeep, pulled into the clearing, jumped out and grabbed machetes from under their seats. They immediately fell to cutting branches and saplings. Within minutes, the entry to the clearing was hidden beneath artfully arranged brush. The clearing was now our private Shangri-La.

David grabbed my arm and gestured towards the first jeep. I nodded and we began unloading the camping gear. It was impressive stuff.

"You guys must have bought out the local store," I gasped at David, between arm-filled trips from the jeeps to the small spring at the middle of the clearing.

"No, we brought it all from Israel. Lots of good gear there. Camping is kind of a national obsession."

"Really? I thought the Israeli national obsession was fighting Arabs."

"Is there a difference?"

Since I had no idea what he meant, I laughed.

These guys were incredibly well organized. Within what felt like minutes, a campsite had been established.

There were two tents. One tent stood by the cooking area, where a small collapsible table had magically appeared. A tarpaulin hung over the table. Even though a propane stove sat on the table, a small fire pit had been dug and lined with stones.

The other tent, at some distance from the first, was near the jeeps. Two more tarps covered the vehicles.

Bernie and David took on the role of cooks. Soon they had a hearty stew working as well as a pot of water for strong, sweet coffee, which would be made and served Greek style: grounds in the cup.

We sat on various outcroppings of rocks to eat. There was a buzz of insects and the smell of flowers in the air. "This place is beautiful," I opined between sips of dark brown nectar. My full stomach and the floral odor lulled me towards sleep. My eyelids drooped.

Where had we been? How old? Family vacation?

It was a hazy memory. My brother skipping stones into a lake. Mom and Dad, their feet dangling in the water, talking low, but happy.

"Hey, Nick, want to do some exploring?" Matt broke into my reverie.

My eyes snapped open. "Sure."

"After dessert."

"Dessert? You guys travel right."

Canned peaches and cookies, some of the stuff Matt and I had bought that morning. These washed down by more of the thick, strong, sweet, coffee.

I assumed we would all go for a hike, but it was Matt, Abe, and myself who formed the "scouting expedition" as Bernie termed it.

"Hey, Mo, want to join us?" I asked.

"Nope. Sorry, Nick, I have some letter writing to do, and my journal's not up-to-date."

"You keep a journal?"

"We all do," David answered for him. "It's another of our national obsessions."

"Maybe I—"

"Let's get a move on," Abe called.

A journal would have to wait. I grabbed my camera and followed the other two along a foot trail leading away from the campsite and towards a strangely shaped outcropping.

Matt led the way. He carried a machete, which he wielded with practiced swings at any vines or branches that blocked the path.

"Watch for snakes," Abe muttered. I was not sure if he was serious. I found myself starting nervously at every vine.

What is that? Is that one? What was that sound?

My mind filled the jungle with danger.

Damn. Good thing I'm with these guys.

Chapter 4: Is It Safe?

We left the jeeps in a clearing and took yet another hike. There had been quite a few of these "side hikes" as Matt called them. "Practice for the Inca Trail," was Bernie's justification.

Too much for me. Feeling physically overwhelmed, I wanted to head back to Lima and from there back to that suddenly attractive pensione in Santiago. Had I been on my own, but, I wasn't.

The steep narrow pathways that exhausted and terrified me didn't daunt my Israeli friends. In the ever-thinning air of the Andes, they talked and sang while I gasped and panted to keep up.

From time to time, they would mercifully stop. These breaks were clearly for me. They kept careful watch over my increasingly labored breathing, often asking how I was doing.

What am I, an experiment, a goyishe lab rat?

Whatever their concern, it didn't keep them from jibing at me. I was younger than them. They should have been struggling to keep up with me. I was obviously out of shape.

"Too many of those happy meals," Abe suggested.

"Cheeseburgers and fries," Matt added.

Is this their motivational technique? What are they telling me? That I should have joined the army instead of coming to Peru? Enough.

"How do you guys do this?"

"We've done some mountain climbing," David, appreciating my desperation, gestured another stop.

I dropped my daypack to the ground. "Another national obsession?" I joked.

"No, a personal one, just us," Abe answered.

"You guys—" My lungs burned with protest.

"When you're surrounded by enemies, when war is always moments away, you learn to savor life," Abe answered an unasked question.

My words came slowly, punctuated by gasps. "Americans don't. We're different. At least now. War. Nobody wants to pick a fight with Uncle Sam. Everybody loves us."

David laughed. "That's the dumbest thing I've ever heard."

Offense showed on my face while I fought to ignore my own experiences in Santiago.

"Look, I'm sorry," David said. "I didn't mean to insult you, but haven't you gotten the message here in South America?"

"What message?"

"Most of the world hates the U.S."

"No way."

"Yes way. The States get more than your share of everything. You push other countries around. And, worst of all, in the Middle East, you usually support us."

"Us?"

"Israel. The Arabs hate us for existing and you for supporting our right to exist. They call you 'The Great Satan.'"

I chuckled. "The Great Satan? I like that. It has a ring."

"What's so funny?" Mo had come up behind me.

"Calling the States 'The Great Satan.' Who the hell believes in Satan?"

"The Muslim world, and you Americans better not forget it."

"You guys aren't fooling around, are you?" There was a funny feeling in the pit of my stomach, a feeling I had felt before. Before Paul, before the houseboat and Key West. When my parents would go at it. Mom shrieking that Dad was a bastard, a whoremonger, and other shitty things. She'd start throwing crap everywhere, all over the house. My brother, if he were home, would slam out the front door. I'd head for my room, turn up my music, and bury my head under the pillows.

It never helped. Mom would storm into my room and insist we had to leave. She'd grab stuff out of my drawers and closet, throwing it in a jumble into a suitcase, all the while screaming and crying great bursts of choking sobs.

The cops would arrive. Dad called them as soon as she started. They'd take her away. A couple of weeks later, she'd be back—chemically relaxed, temper gone, mind slowed, dull, but livable. We'd have peace for a time, maybe a year or even more, but there had always been another round waiting just around the bend. At least until Paul and the divorce.

There were plenty of other kids in school whose parents divorced. I was the only one whose father had custody. I was the only one whose Mom was certified.

Dread lives in the pits of our guts.

Around the campfire, beneath the glistening southern sky, I continued the discussion. I was sure my companions were wrong. Even if the people at the pensione were snots, I was positive the world respected and even loved America.

"Your money," Abe explained in exasperation. "People like your money so they act like they're your friends."

David picked up the thread. "And your government thinks that by offering them money they'll love you."

"That is ridiculous," I countered, "our government does not try to buy—"

They all laughed at once. "What do you think your CIA does?" Bernie asked between chortles.

"The Central Intelligence Agency?" I asked as if I were still in high school.

"Yeah," Bernie sneered, "Your Central Intelligence Agency, what do you think they do?"

"Collect information. You know, spying."

More laughter. The joke was getting on my nerves.

"That's a part of it," David agreed. "But mostly they spread around money and try to buy friends."

"And nobody notices?" I snorted. "You think they can do shit like that without our knowing. I mean, they have a budget. There are auditors. Oversight. Congress."

David laughed even louder. "The money they use doesn't come from any budget. They get their own money."

"What?"

"They make a lot of money doing a lot of things they shouldn't," Mo said.

"Like?"

"Drug smuggling."

"Gun sales." David added.

"Even some legal businesses," Matt put in. "At least they look legit."

I shook my head in resignation. I wanted to argue but had a sense there were facts, lots of facts, I might not, that I didn't know—things I might not want to know. Things these guys did know.

Enough.

"I'm exhausted," I said.

"Yeah. Let's get to bed," Mo agreed.

"I'm just going to have a last smoke."

"You're killing yourself. You know that, don't you, Kid?" Bernie asked.

"Yeah, I know." I pulled out a Marlboro and lit up. I'm going to quit … someday."

"You should." Mo's voice sounded genuine concern.

The next day ever higher. We camped at fourteen thousand feet, just under three miles above sea level: three miles above Long Island, three miles above my heavy-smoking, non-athletic existence.

Sick as hell, I tried to not show it. Waves of nausea and dizziness washed over me. I felt like flotsam off Fire Island, tossing this way and that with each whitecap. The world swam around me. Still, I tried to do some of my share. The others took up the slack, smiled indulgently, and said nothing.

I managed to pick at some dinner, after which Matt suggested another little walk. "It'll do you some good."

"Best thing for you," Mo added.

Every muscle wanted to say no, but I went along. That had become a kind of ritual, three or four of us hiking off from the campsite each evening.

Tired and aching as I was, I determined to keep up. I followed Abe, his machete, as always at the ready, even though there was next to no vegetation at this altitude.

I didn't make it very far. I lagged behind, weaved, and stumbled. It wasn't intentional, it just happened. My mind was trying, but my body had reached its limit. I leaned heavily against a boulder.

Matt and Abe hadn't noticed. I could hear their footsteps moving into the night. I sat on a rock and watched them curve around yet another outcropping and then disappear into the oncoming dark.

I didn't like the solitude or the silence. For the first time in months, I thought about pot, about getting stoned. I wondered if it was possible to feel worse. I wondered if getting high would make things seem better.

Probably not.

At least it might help the damn nausea.

The world spun around me. My eyes focused on nothing.

I better get back. If nothing else, I can take a Tylenol and climb into my sleeping bag.

I shoved myself away from the rock and stumbled along the path, which years of use had worn in the rocks and hard-packed dirt.

It seemed forever. Slightly below and to my left, I saw the rock cairn by which we were camped. I could see them, but the three guys couldn't see me approaching. I must have been pretty quiet because they didn't hear me either.

Rounding a bush, I saw that the back seats of both jeeps had been flipped up. Under each was gear that I hadn't seen before and immediately wished that I never had. There was a small armory: handguns, rifles, shotguns, boxes that probably held bullets and possibly grenades, what I took to be a light machinegun, and a radio.

Holy Christ, what the fuck have I gotten myself into?

Mo looked up from the rifle he was cleaning and saw me. A look of shock crossed his face. He shook his head and gestured me to get away. The gesture was nothing more than a slight movement of his head and eyes, but it felt as if he had threatened me with that rifle. I backed up, more afraid of turning my back on those weapons than I was of walking into one of the poisonous snakes that might inhabit the mountain or of breaking my leg with a careless step.

When the bush was once again between the three men and me, I stopped. I stood in the dark, dripping perspiration even in that dry air, and tried to figure out what was going on.

Mo must have decided to coach me from the campsite. He started to sing. Obviously, it was for my benefit. I waited a moment and started to whistle, softly and then louder. After whistling an entire song, I began another. Then, I came around the rocks as if I had just arrived.

"God, you make a lot of noise," Mo called to me.

"Nobody around to hear me so why not?"

"True."

The weapons had disappeared; the seats were in their normal position.

For whatever reason, Mo had decided to help me conceal my arrival and my knowledge of their dangerous cargo. He had become my ally and protector. I had no idea what that would make me.

That night I shared a tent with Bernie and Abe. We had developed a rotating arrangement for sleeping, one which would, in Bernie's words, allow us to get to know one another better. In all that rotation, there was one unspoken rule, one that I now understood: I never slept in the tent near the jeeps. Lying on the thin foam mat through which I could feel the uneven Peruvian ground, I imagined the others holding weapons at the ready and making clandestine radio reports to … to whom? That was the question.

The answer hit me. I sat bolt upright. Bernie, who was writing in his journal by the light of a Coleman lantern, looked up. "You all right?"

"Yeah, sure." I wondered if my voice came off as reassuring or terrified.

"You're sure?" He sounded uncomfortable. I wondered if he knew what I had seen, if Mo had told him. Maybe he wasn't my protector. Maybe I was going to end up at the bottom of a cliff.

"Of course. I just got an idea." I tried for an unconcerned, easygoing voice.

"Want to share?"

I thought fast. "Just what to get my girl for her birthday."

"And what's that?"

"A miniature of Machu."

"That lame idea got you up in the middle of the night?"

Abe interrupted, "Quiet! I'm trying to sleep."

"Sorry, Abe." I turned back to Bernie. "We can talk about it tomorrow. Probably just the altitude. Makes you think funny. Things go out of perspective. Maybe you can help me think of a better idea."

Yeah, I'm really going to bring back something for Marcie. That would be a mistake, a big mistake.

"Guys!" Abe sounded really pissed.

"Night."

"Yeah, good night."

I lay staring at the blackness of the tent.

Shit. These guys are Mossad. They're fucking Mossad. And, they are trashing the fucking CIA. Shit. Holy crap.

But what the fuck are they doing in Peru? And what the hell do they want with me?

I fell asleep still worrying at those bones and wondering if I really wanted to know the answers.

Chapter 5: Cross Country

Traveling the mountains of Peru I experienced physical difficulties and some anxiety, but I also enjoyed the companionship and camaraderie. Mo had become a very special friend, one willing to protect me. That was a real bond even though I never stopped wondering why he cared about me and what he and the others were up to.

The journey to Machu Picchu became the adventure I had dreamed of sharing with my best friend, Will, the summer we graduated high school.

The town in which Will and I grew up is one of those nondescript endless tracts of middleclass housing without benefit of culture or interest that fill the central portion of Long Island. Once a home for potatoes, ducks, and truck farming, the island had become a pollution-clogged world of automobiles and overly fertilized and poisoned yards. Its own kind of wilderness in which the only surviving animals are Canadian geese who shit green everywhere, raccoons who upset garbage pails, and people, mindless, mind-numbing people.

The teens of Long Island, like teens everywhere, complain of boredom and dream of their futures. Then they stay on, commuting to local colleges, spending their young adult years in their parents' homes, settling into unfulfilling jobs fueled by the colossus that is New York City.

I, too, had spent those high school years complaining of the monotony. Pot had been an easy answer to the tedium. My best friend and marijuana-smoking partner, Will, was an artist by style as well as talent. Longhaired, lanky and Roman nosed, Will wore the second-hand clothes of the hippies who were his role models. Uncharacteristically of our graduating class, Will decided to go far away to a college in the Northwest. The spring of Junior year, his family had flown to Oregon where he fell in love with a small, arts-oriented school.

"Just the kind of place I need," he told me.

"Cool," I answered already missing him and dreading the absence of choices in my life.

The summer of graduation, Will prepared to drive cross-country. He wanted my company, and I wanted to go with him. Neither of us understood that letting go of friends is best done with a sharp knife.

My father, if for no other reason than guilt about Mom, generally tried to be optimistic where I was concerned. His gullible willingness to believe the best was at that moment fueled by my acceptance to Pace and his naïve belief that Will was a good influence. He gave his enthusiastic assent and some financial support.

We allotted six weeks for the trip, enough time to wander, to really get to know the country, and more importantly, to cement our mutual affection against the years ahead.

In preparation for our pilgrimage we read Kerouac. Our discussions were filled with resolutions to travel rough, to get day-jobs here and there, to camp in the most out-of-the-way places we could find, and to sample apple pies until we had found the best in America.

"Why?" I asked about this last goal, which Will had suggested.

"So we can be experts about something. Who knows, Nick, maybe you can write a story for *The New Yorker*."

Why not?

We set off on a hot Monday morning in early July. Will's clothes, books, and have-to-haves were jammed into the trunk of his parents' dented, red Chevy. The back seat was loaded with camping gear, a couple of duffels of clothes, some food, and lots of tapes. Hidden under the camping gear, far from parental eyes, was a plastic baggy filled with weed and four bottles of Jack Daniels, our favorite when we could get somebody to buy for us.

Admonitions shouted and ignored, we were on the way. The Long Island Expressway, the Throgs Neck Bridge, and then the world.

We crossed the George Washington Bridge and hit Route 80. New Jersey hummed beneath us; Black Sabbath surrounded us and we were making good time. Well into Pennsylvania, Will pulled off the highway and onto back roads. Looking for a place to camp, we stopped at a Texaco station and asked.

"There's a state park 'bout twenty miles that way," the attendant told us pointing.

We followed his finger down the two-lane road, through a stretch of woods smelling of pine and country. We found the park. It was full. The ranger told us to try the private campground another five miles down the road.

For twenty-five bucks, the manager assigned us a site. "Fourteen A. Go down here to the second turn, take a left. It'll be on your right. Just the two of you."

"Yes, Sir," Will answered.

"Should be big enough. You'll see the marker. Any questions? You boys follow the rules and you should be just fine."

He handed Will a booklet, which I knew we'd use to start our fire.

We found our site, a small pie-shape wedge cramped between two massive campers, the rolling vacation homes of two large families. The children from both had become mates and ran back and forth through our tiny space playing tag and catch with no concern for our minimalist tent and meager possessions.

I don't suppose the kids meant to be pains in the ass, but Will and I were no longer quite so keen on camping. "Maybe as we get out of the East there'll be fewer people," he said hopefully.

"Sure." I ducked into the tent to take a swig of J.D. The parents of those kids wouldn't care for our drinking or toking in front of their little angels. And, I was pretty sure that both were against those rules, especially since we were underage.

Traveling light as we were, neither of us had brought an air mattress or sleeping mat. I suppose we could have crammed them into the back seat along with everything else, but neither of us wanted to spend the extra money or to think of himself as soft.

Riding through, Western Pennsylvania looks like a green paradise, but it's actually filled with rocks. Lying on them that night, I figured they must be boulders. Neither of us slept well: tossing, turning, and bumping into each other.

Over a breakfast of bad coffee and cold cereal without milk, we decided that from there on we'd stop earlier and be more selective in our camping accommodations. At a groggy six in the morning, those seemed like pretty good solutions to the discomfort of our first night's camping.

The rest of Penn's woods flew by. Ohio followed, then Indiana. We took turns driving. Agreed upon without discussion, neither of us wanted to stop except for a piss, gas, a Coke. For all our Kerouac reading, there didn't seem to be anything worth seeing or doing. Toledo, Columbus, Indianapolis, who cared?

We were just past Chicago. The day was gone. It was unlikely that we'd find a campground. We settled for a motel.

It was a decrepit place, a bunch of cabins built in the Forties. No air conditioning. Insects filled the hot, humid night. They flung themselves against and through the unmended screens. We waved our arms and watched them, ignoring us, dart in and out of the glow of bug-splotched light fixtures.

The shower was one of those narrow white, metal boxes standing on end with a clinging plastic curtain in various shades of faded brown. We waited for hot water to find its way through the compound and then spurt itself at us with clanging and attendant rust.

I dozed fitfully, periodically waking to the buzz and bite of our winged visitors. I'd thrash for a moment then doze again—on and off through the night, too tired to get up and too uncomfortable to sleep. Come the sun, I was more than ready to take off. Will was right behind me.

We stopped at a McDonalds for breakfast, which we declared the first real food we'd had since leaving New York. Back in the speeding Chevy, we shared a gluey fast-food apple pie washed down with chugs of Jack.

Yeah, this is the life.

Freebird pulsed through the sound system.

We were across the river and into Iowa. We plunged in at Davenport, went by Cedar Rapids, charged through Des Moines, and came out at Council Bluff. We stopped at a truck stop to piss, drink coffee, and feed the car. The place was called "Middle America." It sure wasn't any America I recognized, but the burgers were okay. The scraggly-haired waitress asked where we were from and where we were headed and acted impressed when we told her. "I'd love to go to New York."

"Why?"

"'Cause it ain't here."

"Yeah."

"'Cause it … well, it's big."

"Yeah."

We were on a roll, weeks ahead of schedule and moving fast. We had started out in search of America; halfway across the country we had found enough of it that we were in full flight.

The miles rushed beneath us. We took turns driving and sleeping, sleeping and driving—driving as fast as we dared, and sleeping as best we could in the cramped passenger's seat.

Looking back, some nameless terror had taken over and was pushing us like a hapless wheeled beast across the prairies, over the mountains, and eventually to the sea.

My life has often been like that ride. I start with the best of intentions, become obsessed with reaching my destination, and then turn the whole event into a headlong rush toward nothing. The prize of the adventure had become, as so often is the case, not an award, but a farce.

As with all good farce, Will and my "great cross-country adventure" ended with me making a total fool of myself.

We reached Will's college weeks ahead of schedule. It was a lovely place: majestic trees, ivy-covered buildings, manicured lawns filled with handsome young people sporting fashion and spouting the latest middleclass gibberish. The surrounding town offered galleries, coffee shops, and trendy clothing. What more could an art student want?

Will wanted off-campus housing. He found a starving-artist appropriate garret a few blocks walk from the college's arts building. There were plenty of more comfortable rooms available, but Will was determined to get as close as he could to living in Paris, not the Paris of today, but the Paris of Hemingway and friends, the Paris of art and adventure.

More phony apple pie if he asks me.

But he didn't ask.

How he was going to find pre-War Paris in a small, beautiful town not far from the most stunning stretches of the Oregon coast was beyond me. At least he had a dream, which was more than I had.

After helping drag his belongings up the three flights to Will's new hidey-hole, I felt I was due a reward. While he was setting up housekeeping, I downed more than enough of our J.D. and decided that I had to find myself a hooker.

Sex has always been my answer. Not that I was all that experienced in the ways of illicit sex; I had gone to a couple of Times Square peeps and on one occasion bought myself a grand time in a sleazy, rent-by-the-minute hotel. That wasn't where I lost my virginity—that happened at a backyard barbeque—but it was the first time I had really enjoyed screwing.

Sex is a skill like any other. If you want it done properly, hire a pro. The middle-class Long Island dilettante isn't going to do the job right.

I insisted that Will and I drive to Portland to satisfy my desire. He didn't want to, but he could hardly refuse since, as I volubly pointed out, we hadn't exactly done an *on the road* thing and I was due some pleasure in return for sharing the drive.

Will drove. I drank. I finished the J.D. and started on some Rolling Rock we'd picked up to go with a couple shriveled hotdogs at a convenience store in Nebraska. I hadn't eaten since another of our McDonald's breakfasts somewhere in Eastern Oregon, so I was already lightheaded and getting good and blitzed. We found the Greyhound bus station, which figured to be the local equivalent of Times Square. The area looked the part: seedy, full of swaggering women, and homeless drunks. I told Will to slow down and start trolling.

There were a few tarts wandering the street and waving to passing motorists. Not New York City on New Year's Eve, but it would do. Will pulled over. Two girls with everything on display asked if we wanted to party. Will looked at me. I managed to drawl out that I sure did.

"What about you?" one of the girls winked at Will.

"No thanks." He sounded shy, almost tongue-tied. "My buddy, he does."

"Do you want both of us or just one?" the same hooker turned her eyes to me.

"I'm game. Let's do it!" It was pretty obvious I was drunk as hell. Both women laughed.

"What the hell," the first one said.

"Sure thing, big boy," the second added. "There's a nice hotel around the corner."

Will cut the motor and said he'd wait.

"How much?" he asked knowing I was beyond thinking.

"Seventy-five."

Will started to haggle. I cut him short and reached for my wallet.

He pulled the wallet from my hand, counted out the seventy-five, and tucked it into my shirt pocket. "Just in case," he commented softly but loudly enough for the girls to hear.

"What do you think, that we're gonna roll him?"

"Let's just say I'm taking away the temptation."

"That's bullshit!"

"We come from New York," I offered as a drunken explanation. I was already out of the car and standing, half askew, held up by the hood.

"That's nice. I was there once. Went up in one of those big buildings."

"The Empire State?" Will asked.

"The other one. The big one."

"World Trade Center."

"Right. That was it."

They were making small talk, and I wanted to get laid. "Come on," I slurred at the girls.

"Yeah. Sure," one answered, her voice uninterested, we might as well have been on Ninth Avenue.

The first girl was wearing a pink blouse. Its front was tied up to reveal her navel and opened from the top to show her bra. In my stupor, I made a grab for her.

"Hey, look at that, Will, a giant butterfly."

I stumbled forward and landed on one knee.

The other girl grabbed me and laughed. "Come on, butterfly hunter. We'll see if you got a pole to go with your net."

I laughed with them. Leaning on their shoulders, I dragged myself into a slummy hotel. Strips of much-used flypaper hung in the lobby, a lobby furnished for a convention, perhaps an invasion, of lice. The one exception was the new, color television, which the clerk was watching.

He barely nodded to the girls. They pulled me up a flight of stairs, down a dark corridor lined with peeling paint, and into a dingy, scantily furnished, and un-cleaned room.

I managed to get my clothes off and claw at theirs. One of them pulled a pint bottle from her bag and took a swig. I reached out for the container.

"Want some more, Honey?" She handed me the bottle.

It tasted like gin. I never liked the taste of gin so I only took a couple of gulps, which was a lot more than I needed. She took back her bottle. "You're a real drunk, ain't you?"

"No, I usually—"

"Yeah, sure. Look, you paid, it ain't my job to judge." She pushed me backward onto the unmade bed. Both girls piled on top of me and started touching and tickling.

I was excited. I was horny. I was impotent. I just couldn't get it up. I knew it was the booze, but it was still a great metaphor.

All the dreaming, wishing, or bragging in the world doesn't cut the mustard, nor bring the climax.

Worse, they started laughing, laughing at me. If there is anything in the world more embarrassing than being laughed at by a whore, it's being laughed at by two whores. Hands down it became the most embarrassing moment of my life.

The two hookers saw I was upset and tried to calm me. Blaming the alcohol. Reassuring me I could come back another time.

Their reassurances just made the situation worse. I felt like a little kid being placated. I damned them both, half pulled on my clothes, and headed out of the room.

My anger made me feel sober, but my body knew better. I bounced off walls and doors, disturbing other whores and johns, creating a trail of yells, jeers, and profanity behind me.

I got to the stairs, staggered twice, and fell. I bounced and somersaulted down the flight of steps.

The two hookers had followed me out of the room. I'm sure they took a moment to debate going out the emergency exit before coming to my rescue. The two girls carried and dragged me to the car and stuffed me into the back seat. Before Will could say a thing, they slammed the door and took off, with my money, which I must admit they had earned.

I passed out, leaving Will to decide what to do with my battered body.

I woke up the next morning still in the back seat of that damned Chevy. Will was nowhere to be seen, but I recognized the street. He had gone back to his new place. Wincing with pain, I got out of the car. A sprained ankle and a few bumps and bruises, but with the luck of the puking-sick drunk, I'd escaped major injury. My shoes, socks, and underwear were on the car's floor, thrown there by the two women. My clothes were covered with my vomit. The car reeked. I reeked I felt like retching again.

Nice!

I heaved into the gutter.

Chapter 6: Learning the Alphabet

"Yeah, I was born in Puerto Rico, but I don't remember it, not from then. I've been back to visit. My family lives in Ponce; I go to visit. But me? I'm a New Yorker, grew up here, a Hundred and Third and Saint Nick. Mixed neighborhood: Blacks, Puerto Ricans, a few old Jews left over from the fifties."

Jose Figurés leaned back in his desk chair, probably a leftover from the Sixties. Scuffed and squeaky: the condition of the entire Latino Community Center office. Everything either donated or scavenged, a no-frills venture.

Figurés was a no-frills guy. He was giving me his version of how things were. I took notes and kept reminding myself that there was a story, a real Pulitzer winning kind of story, to be had. I wasn't sure where or how I would get it published. It certainly wasn't anything the local weekly I worked for would run, not even if it had been happening in Queens and not Manhattan. I'd been up front with Jose about that. He didn't care. He needed somebody to listen, somebody to write the story down, somebody to make it seem like he wasn't just charging at windmills.

"I don't want to be a Puerto Rican Don Quixote." His fingers drummed a merengue; pencils danced in the Mets cup that served as a holder.

"It was no fun time. I gotta tell ya. Gangs? Yeah, we had gangs. Bopped and fought. Bopped and fought. No drugs, though. Never did no drugs, not as a kid.

"In Nam. That was different. We all did. Only way to stay sane. Shit, that was a no sane war. What the hell were we doing there? It wasn't like everything was great here. There was lots that needed doing right in New York, and I was in fuckin' Vietnam, naked as a blue jay, running around a fuckin' artillery post in the middle of nowhere. Only way to keep the vermin off, run around naked with our balls hanging out. I gotta tell ya, those Cong pajamas were better than our pay all-kinds-of-crap-to-big-business uniforms. I tell ya, those Vietnamese were a shitload smarter than the Pentagon."

He stopped for a moment, took off his thick, dark-framed glasses, and rubbed his eyes. I could see the weariness. Even without the glasses, his eyes had that ringed raccoon look. I jotted a note about trying to carry the sins of the world.

"Carry a notebook. Keep taking notes," my editor had said. It was one of the few things she said that actually made sense to me.

"At least when I got back there was money for school. Took some classes at City College. Lots of bullshit. Teachers who didn't know one end of a rifle from the other preaching about the war, a few talking about Blacks and their rights. Not much about us P.R.s. I gotta tell ya, it seemed like a waste, but Maria, she insisted I stick with it. She was working for transit. We were living together in the projects in Queens, planning to get married. And, she's tellin' me I've got to get school, make something.

"I got to tell ya, I must have been real in love 'cause I stuck. I stuck with her and I stuck with school. I was working part-time at Macy's. Can you believe it? Me selling clothes?"

Figurés laughed derisively as he gestured at his own wardrobe of combat pants, hiking boots, and flannel shirt.

I smiled back with a nod of encouragement. He turned away to look at some papers.

"So, how did you end up here?"

"Oh, yeah. Things were heating up in this part of town. People were squatting in empty buildings, getting them into pretty good shape, too. There were big gatherings in the park, which made the city uneasy. Empty lots were becoming community gardens. There were real winds of change. The whole thing had City Hall worried.

"It wasn't just P.R.s or Blacks or any one group. It was like a revolution, a quiet revolution. I gotta tell ya, the city fathers were crapping their pants. They started cracking down. Somewhere in the aftermath of cracked skulls and all that shit, an idea was taking root, the idea of a community, *comunidad*.

"Well, I got to tell ya, there I was, studying community development and social work. This was a real world lab made to order. One of my professors was talking about it. He was coming down here doing surveys, running back to his ivy-covered world to write papers.

"Me, I came down, too. Started hanging out, taking notes, getting to know players. Made a lot of friends. We got to talking about needing a center, a place the community could meet, plan, do stuff, organize itself.

"David and I had been close in junior high. Hadn't seen each other for years. Serendipity: two old buddies meet down here. He's got lots of friends, and I got lots of friends. Together, shit, we had a ton. I'm pushing the idea of a center and David, well, he's supporting me. Then the city says we can have this empty school. At first there was nothing official like a lease or nothing. Just kind of an agreement. I guess the mayor, the last guy, figures getting some organization down here would make it easier to deal. Might get him some votes, too.

"I got to tell ya, he was right on both counts. Suddenly, people started saying good things about him. Of course, it helped that he told the cops to back off." Jose laughed again, that big, infectious bass laugh, the one that always brought smiles and nods.

"The cops weren't so keen, 'specially when The Latin Kings started hangin'. They had a reputation and rightly so. It was a prison gang, started Upstate 'cause of the supremacists and the Blacks. Sing-Sing survival. Least that's their version. Started in prison and spread to the barrio, which included Alphabet City."

The phone rang, drawing my attention away from Jose's careworn face to his cluttered desk. Papers everywhere. A dirty coffee mug. A takeout cup half filled with milk-tan brew. A can of Coke. Part of a sandwich. A windup alarm clock. Folders and more folders.

Helen, Jose's secretary, dressed in a dark green pencil skirt and white, silk blouse that gave more than a hint of the tight breasts beneath, came in. "It's the city counsel's office." Her voice was guaranteed to make me horny.

"Sorry, Nick, gotta take this one."

I started to get up; he motioned me to stay where I was.

"Hi, Sidney. What's his honor got to say?" There was a pause.

"Tell him to go to Hell. No, better not. Tell him we'll go to court. He can't just dump us out on the street." Another pause.

"The hell he can. We'll fight." He slammed the receiver down. Pens and pencils jumped and clattered.

"That damn son of a bitch. He let the Italians keep their center just below Houston, but this place he wants to sell using *sealed bids*. You know it's gotta be rigged."

"For who?"

"The same bastards that are knocking down everything else around here. They're going to put in co-ops and apartments with just the legally required minimum of low-income stuff. I gotta tell ya, damn thing is none of it will stay standing."

"What?"

"Haven't you figured it out yet? I thought you were a bright kid. They bang on some building on Fifth Street and buildings are swaying all the way down to First." He slammed his hand down on his chaos-covered desk. This time folders, papers, pens, even the telephone, jumped. A photograph fell over and he repositioned it.

"This isn't like the rest of Manhattan. We're sitting on quicksand here. I got to tell ya, there's no bottom, no rock, just landfill and years of silt dumped by the river. They'll put up those big buildings and the whole damn thing will fall down around the poor fools who buy in."

"No shit?"

"No shit, man. Absolutely no shit."

"Don't they know?"

"Of course they know, but ask me if they give a damn. They're using federal and state funds to build with minimum down. They have a state mortgage program ready to assist first time buyers and a federal one for the rest. They'll build as many as they can as quick as they can. By the time the first building sinks up to its asshole or falls on a street, they'll have their money safely tucked away in the Caymans, and they haven't even broken any laws ... unless you count the bid rigging."

His fingers were back to their dance rhythm.

"So what will stop them?"

"Us. The community. And the courts. I gotta tell ya, we've got a right to maintain this place. We live here, man. We'll get another injunction."

"Another?"

"Sure another. We've gotten a few. A couple they ignored—started demolishing at the crack of dawn before the papers could be served. Some they went back to court; got them thrown out. But, we'll keep fighting, stalling them. I gotta tell ya, their whole plan rests on getting as many lots under construction as they can before anything much is completed. Get it all sold before it starts crumbling." Again, he whacked his hand down on the desk. The same photograph toppled, Figurés, his arm around a woman. He picked it up and stared.

"Nick, I gotta tell ya, once it starts the whole thing's a house of cards.

"Our plan's simple, keep 'em in court. Keep them from getting buildings started, at least the ones we can. When shit starts to happen, like buildings leaning over or caving in, then they'll be out of here."

"What about the permits, the city departments? How do they get away—"

"No one can prove it, but the mayor's in bed with them."

"I thought he was law and order."

"Law and order, in the papers, yeah, sure. Reality? Now that's something else. Oh, he went after the mob, or at least one family. Trouble is, he's connected." Jose looked at me with a sly smile and a wink. "He's just connected to a different family."

"Jesus." We were talking about heavy shit, the kind of shit that could get somebody killed. Aren't you afraid?"

"Some. The Latins got my back."

"The Latin Kings? From what I hear they aren't what you'd call the good guys."

"Don't believe everything you hear, Nick. They just want their piece."

"Piece?"

"Of the pie, man. Of the God-damned American pie. Isn't that what we all want?"

"I guess. I kind of grew up with my piece already on my plate."

"So what are you doing here?"

"I told you. I'm a reporter, and you, sir, you are a fucking great story."

"For some dumb-ass weekly in Queens."

"Not my dream to stay there forever."

"So, when push comes to shove, you want more. Maybe you want your piece, too?"

"Yeah, I guess I do."

Chapter 7: On Hold

The era of Marcie was ending. Melinda's time was just beginning. Marcie didn't want to go back to Santiago. I can't say I blamed her. Chile might have a decent economy and quality of life, but the States are the States, and New York is The Big Apple.

She may not have wanted to go back to Chile, but I was certainly ready for Marcie to get on that plane. Our life together was already on the skids when I met Jose. At least before that earthshaking day, with only a part-time job and very occasional attendance at school, I had plenty of time left over for Marcie, a lot more time than I wanted to give. Once I hooked up with Jose and started following him around doing my research for that Pulitzer, well, Marcie—good old, sex-starved, boring Marcie—had no chance.

"*¿Ya no me ama mass? Nick?*" she'd plead.

"*Estoy ocupado.*"

"*Siempre dices estar ocupado.*" That was true, where she was concerned, I was always busy.

Besides, there was Melinda. She taught preschool at the community center and helped Helen, who packed a week's work into every day and needed all the help she could get.

Incredibly sweet, and easygoing, Melinda's attitude rubbed off on everyone; she brought smiles to lips and laughs to hearts. She also had an hourglass body, could kiss like no one I had ever met before, and best of all, rumor was she gave great head. That was a story I wanted to check out first-hand.

I wasn't Melinda's kind of guy, not even close. I was just one of the drooling idiots who followed her around and helped out with the little ones as an excuse to be near her.

In some ways, Helen was sexier than Melinda; she gave off exotic vibes of erotic promises and secrets. Too bad she was a relationship kind of woman. Besides, Helen mooned after Jose. No way was I getting any action.

Melinda gave off different vibes of fun and accessibility. I didn't want to work at a relationship. I just wanted to enjoy, which, even without adding in the Jose effect, made fun and accessibility the winning ticket.

Between constantly bombarding Jose with questions for a story yet-to-be-written and drooling after Melinda, I spent hours at the center, which meant I was pretty much leaving Marcie alone for hours in my dingy, studio apartment.

What else could she do? She called her furious father, whose opinion of *Yanquis* in general and *this Yanqui* in particular was deep in the sewer. Angry as he had every right to be at her and certainly at me, he did as every good father would; he bought her a ticket back to Santiago.

I didn't want to, but I gave in to Marcie's pleading and went to J.F.K. with her, even though it meant paying for the cab and helping her with her bags. With nothing to say, we stared through each other. I waited around for an everlasting hour, shared a quick peck, and watched until she got past security.

What the hell, I might as well.

With a sense of relief, I returned her wave. Finally, I could go home. Without Marcie waiting for me, I wanted to be there.

When I got back to my place, I found Marcie's note. She still loved me. She wished I still loved her. It was really sad, but I didn't feel like crying. I felt liberated. I felt like celebrating. I felt like getting laid.

I took a chance and called Melinda. "I'd really like to see you."

"Oh?"

"Marcie left today."

"Oh."

"Kind of feeling down."

Lies are easy, especially when they'll work.

"I understand," she said.

"Real lonely."

"Why don't you come over for a drink?"

A stroke of luck. Melinda seldom had an evening free, and there she was, waiting for me to call. Bus, subway, and I rang her bell.

There are lots of shades of pink: rose pink, hot pink, dusty pink, flesh pink, coral pink, salmon pink, carnation pink, even fuchsia pink. I'd never seen pink like the teddy Melinda was wearing. It was sheer, sheer enough I could see her already aroused nipples beneath.

Hot damn.

Instantaneously hard, I had trouble making it through the door.

"You like it?" she asked with a knowing, mocking smile. Her lips were the same color as her lingerie.

"Of course." I licked my chops, staggered to her sofa, and fell into it.

"Some wine?" The bottle and glasses were on a small marble-topped table.

"Sure."

How about some sex first?

She poured two glasses of red and slithered across the rug towards me. "Take off your jacket."

"Yeah, sure." So turned on, I hadn't remembered I was wearing a parka. I managed to get it off without really standing up. She handed me one of the glasses, took my jacket, and carelessly flipped it onto a nearby chair.

"Your hat, too."

I tossed my blue balaclava onto the jacket and watched it slowly inch downward, pick up speed, and fall to the floor.

Melinda sat next to me and took a sip of wine. I took a sip, too, a big one.

She took my glass and set it and her own on the coffee table. Moved closer. I squirmed with anticipation.

Melinda smiled. I smiled back. In that moment she had wrapped herself around me.

The next morning I awoke with a mouth full of cotton and a splitting headache. That was okay with me. After all, I was waking up in Melinda's bed. I watched her dress, each movement a new temptation.

Melinda delicately moistened those delicious lips with her tongue. "That was fun."

"It sure was."

I must be the luckiest bastard in the world. Good sex, great fun, excitement, and best of all, no Marcie.

There followed a series of nights at Melinda's. Some mornings I could barely walk, but they were happy nights.

While my life was on sex-gorged hold, things in Alphabet City were getting worse. Jose was frantically busy. He was trying his damnedest to come up with ways to stop the city from selling the school building that was now the community center's home. If it took place, the sale would be by means of a closed-bid auction. Besides constantly barraging the media and filing court documents, Jose and David were trying to raise money for a bid. If they couldn't stop the city from auctioning the building, Jose would try to buy it on behalf of the Latino community. That meant coming up with ten percent of the bid in cash from a community where most people didn't have the price of a plate of *arroz con frijoles*.

To make Jose's job harder, the court cases were assigned to Judge Joe Solomon, a son-of-a-bitch with very little wisdom. His Honor also happened to be the mayor's best friend and one of the finance chairmen on the mayor's election campaign. Since Jose's lawsuit was nominally against the mayor, the judge should have recused himself.

Should have doesn't cut it in politics.

His Honor didn't see any conflict of interest. "Señor Figurés, I trust you are not questioning this court's impartiality," he said from the bench. "Justice must be blind. It would be a sorry state of affairs if you were to feel it was otherwise."

Sure, and no ethnic bias either; right, Señor Judge?

"I'm impartial and objective," Solomon responded to one reporter as he left the court building on a chilly, rainy day. He hadn't bothered to add that he was on his way to meet the mayor for lunch.

And, all the while, the wrecking balls were swinging. Day after day, buildings crumbled and shook. The building that housed my one-room hole got bad enough that I decided to bail before it buried me along with the roaches. I felt bad doing it, like I was running away, like I was letting Jose down, like I was letting the community down, like I was letting myself down. At the same time, I had no wish to die in a pile of dust, bricks, and debris.

I found an apartment share across the East River in Brooklyn Heights. It was an old, grey stone building, reasonably genteel, mostly rent-controlled, leases passed from family member to family member. One of my new roommates had inherited the lease on this three-bedroom apartment and its moldering furnishings from his aunt. The other roomy was a grad student trying to survive on a fellowship. They were friendly enough, although Jay, the grad student, was gay and kept giving me the eye. He was just another reason for spending as many nights at Melinda's as I could.

When she wasn't with another guy from her personal posse of admirers, Melinda was always hot and ready. No rules, no pretensions, just fun. She was a young nympho-man's dream. To make things even better, she had money, the serious family kind that makes New York fun.

Working at the community center was just one more way Melinda had of making her life interesting. Whether she was working in the preschool, helping Helen, flirting with the guys, or sitting in a meeting with Jose and David, Melinda always enjoyed herself. When we were eating at a restaurant—her treat since I had no money—making out in the park, or making like bunny rabbits under her sheets, she was happy and we were flying high.

Chapter 8: Connected

Looking back, my dad was a natural boy scout, maybe not in his marriage, but in his dealings with the rest of the world. He had had his share of chances to get *connected*. The mob wanted him to launder money. The family parking garage, the one he'd been left by his father, was right near Wall Street. Five days a week it did a hefty business. Saturdays were a slower, which is why my brother was allowed to work Saturdays once he had his license and was old enough to be covered by the business's insurance. Sundays, Dad didn't bother opening, at least not after Mom left.

Before that, when I was a little kid, he was almost never home. Mom claimed, in stentorian screams, he was whoring around. He said he was working. The truth: he had a comfortable hidey-hole office at the garage. I never met any of his girlfriends before Mom left, but it wouldn't surprise me to learn that for all the hysterics she'd been right.

Crazy is often a family affair.

I don't actually know the facts. It's hard to say what the rights and wrongs of their marriage were. By the end she'd gone over the edge — or off to Key West, which was the same thing — and he no longer gave a damn.

My brother Jim, four years older than me, is pretty much a waste-case. He never got by the drug thing, probably because he started drugging with our mother. He still sees her regularly and comes back wasted and angry. He doesn't see much of Dad, just when he wants money. Then he enjoys a free steak and a few crisp Benjamins.

Two years after Jim started working at the garage, Dad announced that he had to stop and that I would never begin. Both of us made a big adolescent stink, screaming that he should treat us like the adults we weren't.

At the time, I thought he was being a tight-ass. After all, I was an adolescent, thought I knew everything, and that every adult was a hypocrite. Looking back, I feel like a damn fool.

That's because now I know the whys. The Puglese family was trying to move in on him, to take over the business. Jim and I would have been hostages in the negotiations.

The Pugleses made some heavy threats.

The old man said, "The hell with you," and took to carrying a gun. He also hired some ex-cons to work for him, the kind of guys you don't mess with.

The Pugleses sent a couple of their enforcers around to intimidate Dad. When the two hoods got out of the hospital, they moved to Vegas. Of course, I learned all of this later, when Dad wanted to unload to someone he could trust and we were sharing the overpowering sense of awe that's Easter Island.

"I didn't say anything at the time, didn't want you and Jim worrying, but I wasn't sure how it was going to end.

Bullshit! You put made men in the hospital.

"But I was acting tough. No other way to do it. Hell, I even sent them flowers, big arrangements, one to each of those hoods while they were recuperating. Figured that was mob style. Maybe I'd just watched too many movies."

Dad pulled out his wallet and extracted two pieces of paper—the receipts for those flowers. He'd kept them as souvenirs.

A hundred bucks each.

Then, I knew he was telling the truth. I respected the old man a lot more after that. I guessed the mob did, too.

I thought about Dad's story while Jose was telling me about the bribe he had refused. He and David, his buddy and assistant, had been offered a hundred grand apiece if they'd just walk away from the center and let the building go up for auction. David had been all for taking the money, but that wasn't Jose's style. In a way, he was very much like my old man, another natural boy scout.

The gangster who approached Jose and David was also a Puglese, Johnny "Two-Fingers" Puglese.

Jose explained, "We called him 'Two-Fingers' because he'd blown the other three off his right hand with an M-80. That was when we were kids on the Upper West Side. I gotta tell ya, there was this Jewish tailor who wasn't paying protection, so big Anthony, Johnny's father, tells him to take care of it. We were in seventh grade. Which that makes us, what? Eleven? Twelve?

"I guess the old man figured it was time for Johnny to learn the family business. He was supposed to throw this M-80 into the guy's shop. I gotta tell ya, Johnny wasn't the brightest bulb in the pack. He holds onto the M-80 and blows off his damn fingers.

"When he hears the noise, the tailor comes out of his shop to see what's going on. There's Johnny lying on the ground and screaming his head off. So the old guy takes him to the hospital.

"The doctors say the tailor maybe saved Johnny's life. Old Man Puglese tells the tailor he don't have to pay protection anymore. He gets it free.

"Now, Johnny's a made-man, maybe even a capo. But, I gotta tell ya, he's still dumb as shit, too damn dumb to make it very far up the ladder, even if the ladder belongs to his old man. But the family is still taking care of him.

"Anyway, since he knows, well, knew, David and me years ago, back in junior high, the Pugleses pick him to make us the offer."

Jose's fingers drummed on the desktop. He was smoking one of his favorite cigarillos; smoke cascaded out of his mouth and nose with every word. I had a Marlboro going. Between us, we had the room filled. It was getting hard to breathe. I was almost wishing Helen would come in and interrupt us, but she was at the Clerk of the Court's office filing yet another of the endless stream of papers that Jose and his lawyer-friend, Mike Jacobs, were creating almost daily. They knew that Judge Solomon would find something wrong with each filing, or some reason that their motions shouldn't be granted, but they kept at it anyway.

"I got to tell ya, I didn't know whether to consider it a compliment that they went with an old sort-of-a-friend, or whether it was an insult that they didn't use somebody with half a brain. What I did know was that there was no way I was taking their bribe."

Jose took a few machine-gun drags on his cigarillo. He coughed a couple of times. Even his lungs had limits. "David wanted to take the money and run. *Damn*, that makes me mad. There's no way."

He paused for a bit and I got a few words in, "Why is the mob involved? I thought this was a bunch of the mayor's business friends."

Jose shot me a look. "Who the hell do you think His Honor's business friends are?"

"Yeah" I stammered. "I just thought … with his whole reputation … I figured he kept those guys in the shadows."

"Quite a world isn't it?"

"But the developers have to be checked out, vetted, or some such thing?"

"Of course, and they look clean. The mob's in the background, but who the hell do you think runs the construction companies, the demolition companies, the damn unions? I gotta tell ya, they find some front men, a few *honest* businessmen, and away they go."

"Shi-it."

"Want to know the best part?"

"Sure."

"The top bid on this building isn't from one of their guys. There's this guy, Hunter. He bid, high, won. But the thing is nobody seems to know who this Mr. Hunter is. No connection to the Mayor's office. No connection to the mob. Least none anybody finds. I mean, Nick, the guy is a cipher."

"How did that happen?" I prompted him.

"Look at the bidding. Ever notice that the winning bid on every piece of property the city has sold was just slightly higher than the administration wanted? Ever notice that the sale prices on the private buildings haven't really been going up? This has been a *controlled market*, a very *controlled market*."

"Yeah? So how did Hunter get into the game?"

"I don't know. Nobody seems to know. Maybe he just lucked in. Maybe he got a mole inside and figured out what to bid. Either way, I gotta tell ya he'd better be careful or he'll end up wearing cement."

"A beach party in the East River?"

"Or the landfill on Staten Island. Who knows? Maybe they'll put him with Jimmy Hoffa."

"So what do you think his game is?"

"Oh, Hunter, he'll sell out, sell to Puglese. But he'll get a little extra to keep him quiet."

"Or he's dead meat?"

"Or he's dead meat."

The intercom buzzed. "Yeah," Jose rasped into his end.

Melinda's distorted voice came from the other end. She was covering for Helen. "There's a Mr. Hunter here. He wants to talk with you."

"Tell him to go to hell." Jose stopped to think, "No, better, tell him to come on in."

I started to get up. "Where are you going?" he growled.

"I figured I would be in the way."

"That's your job. You're a damn reporter aren't you?"

I nodded.

"Then you be in the way. Let's see if the glare of publicity makes our Mr. Hunter run for cover."

Melinda brought Hunter in. A tall, thin man made conspicuous by the thick, frameless glasses which gave him an owlish appearance, a visual effect intensified by the widow's peak of his jet-black hair.

As he came through the door, Jose got up, his hand outstretched. "So, Mr. Hunter, we finally meet."

Jose turned to me, "I'd like you to meet a friend of mine. He's a reporter with …"

Chapter 9: Reunion

Melinda and I were at My Lady, Melinda's favorite sex-goddess boutique. Like most guys, I'm not wild about shopping, but this was something *droolingly* different. My birthday was coming up and Melinda was looking for just the right present. She'd asked what I wanted and, truthfully, I'd told her she was more than enough. She, in turn, insisted my gift had to have the perfect wrapping.

There we were, looking for the wrapping. Melinda was prancing around pulling dainties off the shelves with the intensity of a lioness hunting for the best haunch of eland. Holding each piece against her body, she'd whirl around so I could appreciate its full gasping effect. The more she whirled, the harder I got. I was ready to rip through my jeans. Standing, shifting, one foot on top of the other, embarrassment, hiding my engorged prick from popular view.

Middle school relived on Park Avenue.

Knowing how I was reacting was half the fun for Melinda. She'd dance by and touch my sensitivity with her fingertips. With each touch I fought to hold back a yelp of pleasure, pain, and desire.

That was one thing Melinda especially liked: me yelping.

She came strutting one more time, a few pieces of merchandise tossed over her left arm, a filmy bra dangling from her fingers. With her right hand, Melinda reached out and took the flap of my belt. Using it as a leash, she pulled me towards the dressing rooms.

"Woof," I barked, happy to play the game.

"Come on, Big Dog, let's try these on together."

I saw the salesclerk, thin but muscular, dressed in black leather, watching our every move through tense, slit eyes. "You're kidding, right?"

"Have you ever done it in a dressing room?" She pulled harder.

"No." I licked my lips.

I nodded to the salesclerk. She gave the slightest inclination of her head in response.

What the fuck!

The dressing room was big enough. We were swinging right along and making a fair bit of noise, especially when I was sitting on the little wooden bench and Melinda was bouncing up and down so franticly that I ended up slipping to the floor with a thud.

One of the salespeople knocked on the door. "What's going on in there?" A giggle in her voice.

Well, that isn't Miss Leather.

"Exactly what you think," Melinda called back.

The saleswoman broke up. By the time she'd gotten herself together and was insisting we come out, we were through. And, I was definitely finished.

Needing a smoke, I went outside, leaned against the plate-glass, and lit up while Melinda completed her shopping.

"Hey, man."

I recognized the voice but couldn't place it. I turned slowly like I was just taking in the view. No point looking like a fool if the speaker was greeting someone else.

But, he was talking to me. It was Mo, all dressed up: suit, tie, fancy shoes, the whole works. Not like Peru, but still Mo. My Israeli buddy suddenly appeared in Manhattan.

"How's it going?" He came toward me hand extended. "What are you doing here?"

We shook hands while wrapping our left arms around each other. It felt great to see him. Perfect timing, too. He'd be blown away by Melinda. It feels terrific to have a good-looking woman in tow.

"I'm waiting for my girl to finish shopping." I gestured, in what I hoped was a nonchalant manner, toward the store with its provocative window. "What the hell are you doing here, Mo? Are the other guys with you?"

"Nope. It's just me. I have a job here in New York."

Without thinking, without thought of the *Mossad*, I asked what it was.

"Telecommunications," Mo answered with a shrug that immediately told me he was lying. "You working?"

"Yeah. I have a job on a newspaper, a reporter."

What the hell. We can both lie.

"That's great."

His enthusiasm was real enough to embarrass me. I decided to fess up—at least some.

"Not really. Just on a local weekly, but it's a beginning." Still not discomfited enough to add it was just part-time employment and way underpaid.

Melinda came out with her shopping bag of goodies. I introduced them and yeah, Mo was impressed. Why wouldn't he be? That made my day.

There was a Starbucks nearby. We went for a cup of coffee.

Give me some ratty used-up coffee shop with stale coffee made in giant urns and served in chipped, white mugs anytime, but Melinda liked to feel sophisticated, and Starbucks did the job for her.

We ordered. Mo jumped forward, an impressive wad of bills in hand, to pay for all three of us.

"That's very nice of you. Thanks," Melinda said.

"Yeah," I added, "the telecommunications industry must be doing well." I couldn't help adding a little, annoyed cough.

"I've been meaning to try to find you, but you know how busy things can get," Mo said.

"Sure."

"Anyway, who would have bet that I'd run into you on the streets of Manhattan?" Mo seemed to be in a real up mood. Somehow his cheerfulness was slowly eating away at my feelings of conquest.

Hey, Buddy, she's mine. Melinda is mine.

"The odds must be one in a million," Melinda answered for me.

"Definitely," I muttered.

We drank our coffee. The day was chilly, and the coffee felt good even if it did have that distinctive burnt Starbucks taste.

My lips tightened. My breath shortened. My hands were clammy. Paranoia is one of my basic response modes. Mo wasn't doing anything the least bit out-of-line. Neither was Melinda. Nevertheless, my personal green jealousy monster was working overtime telling me they were on the way to an affair.

The conversation turned to the Community Center and Jose. To my surprise, Mo had heard of both and knew something about the entire

Alphabet City building boom. "Without Burmaste, the mayor wouldn't have been able to take the election."

"That's true," Melinda agreed.

Taken aback. "Who the hell is Burmaste?" I demanded. If my paranoia was running before, now it was in overdrive.

How the hell does Mo know more than I do about the whole thing? How's he involved?

"He runs the Alphabet City Social Club on Fifth Street, and he's the mayor's assistant for appointments," Melinda answered.

"Burmaste ran the Lower East Side campaign for the mayor —"

"And, now, he decides the mayor's political appointees," Melinda finished Mo's sentence.

"How come nobody ever mentioned him before? I never even heard his name."

"He's one guy you don't mention around Jose," Melinda explained. "They hate each other."

"They're bitter rivals," Mo added. "Who's going to win the hearts and minds of the community? That kind of thing."

"Burmaste's as conservative as they come, and, well, you know Jose. He loves people," Melinda said. "Besides, a Cuban and Puerto Rican, like oil and water."

"Bad blood. Lots of bad blood."

"Yeah," I said, "Jose wants to make the world a better place."

"Not by Burmaste's standards. He's a straight law-and-order man." Mo paused for emphasis. "Except when it involves himself."

"Or the mayor," Melinda added.

We stopped talking to get a second round of coffees. I really didn't want any more and while I was learning some interesting shit, I really didn't want Mo and Melinda around each other. My little green jealousy-monster, feasting on Starbucks and conversation, was growing by the minute.

I tried to pay, but Mo muscled me aside, which didn't do my hold on that green monster any good.

"Come on, man," I pleaded. "I'm not indigent."

"Don't worry, I'll write it off. The company will pay for it."

I was thinking of countering that my paper would pay, but I knew they'd both laugh. Local papers covering tiny pieces of Queens don't give their reporters expense accounts.

To make things worse, Mo ordered Krispy Kremes. I couldn't afford to eat a lot of treats.

Damn you.

My mouth was watering.

The combination of smells, rich burnt coffee, sticky sweet doughnut, and jealousy turned me on. I ran my hand up and down Melinda's thigh. She shot me a back-off look, but, paradox that she was, also leaned over and kissed me on the lips. I kissed back, trying to force my tongue into her mouth. Not going there, she pulled away, took a bite of doughnut and a swig of coffee and laughed, an annoyed snickering laugh, the kind of laugh my mother had given when I made funny faces to get her attention. How was I to know that Mom was talking to Paul or even that he existed? How was I to know what voices were playing in her head?

Hurt, but mostly embarrassed, I stood up. "Got to get to work. I have a shit-load of stuff to get in for this week's edition."

That was true enough, but it wasn't anything new, I was always behind at the paper. I just wanted to get the hell out of there. I just wanted to make a dignified retreat.

"It was great running into you." Mo gave me another handshake and hug. He handed me his business card. "That's my cell so you can always reach me."

"Thanks," I got out one of my cards from the paper. It was a generic card, we all carried them, names of the weeklies and office phone. I added my name and my home phone, and handed it to him.

I kissed Melinda. This time she let me get a little tongue action before again pulling back.

"You'd better get going," she said, trying to sound concerned.

I didn't want to leave them together, but I had made my grand, if infantile, gesture and had to live with it.

Grabbing the rest of my French cruller, I headed for the door. As I exited, I pulled my muffler tight around my throat and looked back. They were talking away like old friends.

I threw the uneaten half of the Krispy Kreame into the nearest garbage.

Chapter 10: The Paper

She was pissed. I'd been working at the paper for six months and had never before seen my editor so angry. It was like an old movie, one of those grainy black-and-whites with somebody constantly yelling, "Copy boy. Copy boy," and "Stop the presses." Emily was screaming her head off at the staff, all three of us. Technically, each of us worked for a different neighborhood locale and she was the editor for all three. In reality, we mashed together into one dysfunctional organism.

Her rant was about missing local news and, worse, missing deadlines. "Some of you seem to find Manhattan more interesting than Queens." She sneered directly at me. "Well, I don't blame you, but *The Times* isn't going to hire you. Neither is *The News* or *The Post*. So, you're stuck in Queens with little old me. You know why? Because not one of you is a real reporter. Hell, you can't even write English."

She dumped piles of offending articles on each of our desks. I was relieved that my pile looked smaller than the others'.

"I ought to hire myself a new staff," she mocked.

Yeah, sure, like you could find three suckers who would work for what you pay us.

"I know you all think you'll find a big story somewhere that's going to make you famous. Forget it. There are no big stories hiding out there waiting for unknowns."

I knew she was directing her sarcasm towards me.

What about Woodward and Bernstein?

The other two looked like she was forcing castor oil down their throats. I probably looked the same. I didn't want to hear how I was nowhere and getting there fast. I wanted my damn Pulitzer. That's every young reporter's dream—the big prize-winning story. So what if I was working on a neighborhood weekly? So what if my editor didn't think I could write? I knew that someday my byline would be famous and that Emily's jealousy would fester into an ulcer.

To make the entire operation look bigger and more professional than it was, we used a variety of arbitrarily assigned pseudonyms and shared articles across the three papers. Twelve different regular bylines graced the three papers—none of them our actual names. The same names had preceded all of us, including the editor. They'd still be in use when we had all passed on to hopefully better papers, or at least better paying jobs.

"By the way," Emily continued, "do any of you know how to use spellchecker? I can't believe the mistakes you're making. You're working at a goddamned computer. Don't turn spell check off. I know it catches most of the proper nouns, but so what? While we're on the subject of spelling," she looked directly at me, "try to look out for homonyms. Does anyone know what homonyms are?"

What are we back in third grade? When is the fire drill? Walk single file. No running in the halls.

Pat, easily the head kiss-ass among us, raised her hand.

Jesus, we really are in grade school.

Emily nodded towards her.

Words like hare, here, hair and hear." She spelled each one. "They sound the same, but they're spelled differently."

Emily continued for her. "And, they mean different things, don't they?"

"Different things," Pat repeated.

Emily's voice, more pedantic than any third grade teacher, more grating than my mother's when she was in high rant. I wanted to slap her. I settled for banging the desk drawer closed.

Yep, back in grade school. Me, too.

"And bear, beer, and bare," Pat added ever the good child and ignoring my attempt to disrupt.

Madam Editor was pleased. She loved it when one of us groveled. I wanted to shove a broom up Pat's ass. This time I settled for moving a pile of papers and *accidentally* toppling them to the floor.

I hated Emily's harangues. Worst thing, she was usually right. We were strictly bush-league and she was teaching us, but not how to be real professionals. I could see limits in my own work, but it was hard to write deathless prose about Little League schedules, school lunches, and P.T.A. meetings.

At the moment, I was working on a really fascinating piece about that local Little League. Some of the coaches wanted to trade players, which was against league policy and which was also making for some very upset kids and parents. Talk about major stories.

"Coach Johnson, is it true that the Granger boy played third base for the Bell Chevy Dodgers?"

"Yes." The coach shifted his feet. I wondered if he was planning to make a run for it.

"Can you explain why he's now the star shortstop with the Elmhurst Diner Colts?"

"Well. Uh." The man hemmed and hawed. Finally, he admitted it, the big scoop. "Well, he switched teams."

Investigative journalism at its least.

There was one slightly brighter side to my job: I covered the police precinct, but only for the local stuff. Emily's unofficial motto was, "If it will make it to *The Times*, it doesn't belong on our pages."

Even though it was minor stuff: car crashes, muggings, break-ins, and the like, I really dug the police beat. It made me think of the future, of having a career. I was also making some contacts at the precinct, nothing big, but contacts, guys, officers, those who would actually talk with me.

Frank O'Marra, an overweight caricature of a desk sergeant, occasionally had a beer with me. Mostly he would talk about police procedure and sometimes he'd let me in on some of the dirt: cops screwing behind K-Mart, a low-life, low-level dealer who was allowed to walk in exchange for information, a hooker and a lieutenant who were shacking up, the usual petty crap of a petty world. He shared those stories with a grin that revealed misaligned teeth with lots of fillings.

Every once in a while I would ask Frank to do me a favor, some little bit of information that might improve a story. Sometimes he obliged; most times not. The important thing was that he never took offense.

Most of the few compliments Emily had given me were the results of getting those little details. "Color," she called it.

A mugging: an older woman cashed her Social Security check and was walking home when a teenaged, sweat-shirted hood grabbed her purse. Three good Samaritans came to her aid, grabbed the kid, held him for the cops, and returned her bag.

It was a nice story. I made it better by getting the Samaritans' names, the lady's age, the fact that she had just cashed her check, and the fact that the thug admitted he had been watching her for a couple of months just so he'd get her right after she cashed it. All of which was courtesy of O'Marra. Emily had eaten it up, even writing an editorial warning seniors to vary their routines.

I rewrote the Little League story and then rewrote it again. I was stalling, hanging around the office because I had another favor to ask of Frank and we weren't meeting until six thirty.

This time the favor wasn't for the paper, it was for me. I wanted to find out more about John Hunter, the mysterious, owlish purchaser of the school that housed the Community Center. I had his name, the social security number he'd given with his bid, his address on Riverside Drive, also from the bid documents, and the plate from the black Lincoln Town Car he had driven to the center. Maybe the information would help Jose, maybe not, but I wanted to learn something about the mystery man, about his background, about the source of his money.

"Whadda ya want it for?" was Frank's staccato response. At the same moment he raised his hand to Mahatma and gestured for another beer.

For some reason, Frank liked to do his drinking sitting at the green and gold bar at Sahib Palace, a local Indian restaurant. He and Mahatma had long since become bar stool buddies.

The rest of the precinct favored The Elms, a bar just down the block from their precinct house. Frank only went to The Elms when a major event was taking place: a welcome party for a crew of rookies who had finally won acceptance, a retirement racket, or the death of one of their own.

An oddball among cops, Frank was not big on the close-knit world of blue. Maybe that was why he talked to me. Maybe it was because I would spring for a beer.

"A story," I explained.

Mahatma brought Frank another bottle and looked to see if I needed one. I shook my head and the barkeep went back to mixing drinks for the diners, who half-filled the deep red room, which was redolent with the aromas of India.

"What about?"

"The real estate market."

"So you know he's in real estate. Why don't you just go to the realtors' board?"

"No, he's the money behind the deal, the hidden investor." I hoped that sounded intriguing enough.

"Around here? You've got to be kidding. Nobody needs a money man in this area." Frank took an extra-long swig.

I was hungry. The last thing I had eaten was the beginnings of that Krispy Kreme. The rumbling in my stomach was intensified by those curried smells wafting through the restaurant. I didn't dare spend the little bit of cash I had in my pocket. If Frank said "yes," I'd have to pay for his beer, and he was already on his third.

"Not a local story."

"So, why are you doing it?"

What the hell. Is he working for Emily?

"Because I want a Pulitzer." I threw the line out hoping he'd bite.

"What the hell's a Pulliser?" he asked. "Budweiser ain't good enough for ya?"

"A Pul-it-zer," I said it carefully. "It's the biggest prize in journalism. I want to win one."

"Ya know, Nick, when I was in the service I wanted to win the Medal of Honor. I kept talking about it in basic. One day the D.I., a nasty son-of-a-bitch from Arkansas, but one hell of a soldier with the decorations to prove it, takes me to one side. Now, I'm real gung-ho and I figure he's gonna tell me how great I'm doing.

"Instead he says, 'What the hell are you tryin' to do, boy, get yourself killed? If you spend your entire career in this man's army peeling potatoes, you'll get to go home to your momma in one piece.'

"Sarge," I say, "I figured I'd be a hero like you. I've always wanted to get me a Medal of Honor.

"Well, he's laughing, and I'm feeling like a total jerk. The worst part is I don't even get the damn joke.

"Finally, he spits it out, 'O'Marra those fools didn't plan it that way, they just got themselves in bad situations. No sane man goes lookin' for a death trap. You gonna come out of your six-by-three to read the commendation? Just find yourself those spuds and keep peeling.'

"And the son-of-a-bitch goes off laughing again.

"I got to see action. First day the guy next to me gets blown to hell. I nearly shit myself. That's when the Sarge's advice hits home. I did my share, but I stayed safe.

"Got back here and I got two uncles and my dad on the force. So I become a cop, too. First chance I get I take the Sergeants' exam. I pass it and get myself a desk. It's safe. Some nut may come in the precinct and blow me away, but for the most part, it's safe. I don't want no Pissiler Prizes."

"Pul-it-zer," I repeated again knowing he was baiting me. "And I do. So will you do me this favor?"

"Yeah, sure, kid." He picked up the paper I had left on the bar. "Give me a couple days."

"Thanks, Frank, I owe you."

"Yeah, ya do, and ya owe Mahatma."

I dug in my pocket and came up with fifteen bucks. It was more than we owed by at least one more bottle. I put it on the bar.

"I gotta get back to work," I lied.

"The hell you do," Frank said through his grin. "You're gonna go bang that girlfriend of yours, and I don't blame ya."

He was right, of course. My next stop would hopefully be Melinda's bed. Those dainties from My Lady had been gnawing away at my insides all day. Besides I wanted to reassure myself that nothing was going to happen between Melinda and Mo.

Chapter 11: Intimidation

I hadn't seen her for a while so I wasn't sure how Melinda was feeling about me. I stopped by the Community Center to say hi. Besides, I hadn't talked with Jose for a few days and wanted to catch up on the latest court battles.

Helen was sitting at her desk, a big dark wooden thing, probably one of the old teachers' desks that came with the building.

"She's not here."

"What about the kids?"

"They're not here either."

"What's going on? She take them to the park or what?"

"Nope. No class today. Nothing." I must have looked as puzzled as I felt because she continued. "Don't you listen to the God-damned news?"

"Not really."

"What kind of reporter are you?"

"If it's already on the radio, there is no reason for me—"

"Bullshit." The word spattered against my eardrum. "So you haven't heard?"

"Heard what?"

"About the raids."

"What are you—"

"She's talking about The Latins. The cops: state, local, and even the feds hit them last night." Jose was standing behind me. "I gotta tell ya, it was like a war, like a military thing."

The Latins are a prison gang, a national organization with a strong chapter in Alphabet City. For all their infamy, The Latins provided a lot of the day-to-day order in the community. Headed by a half-Puerto Rican, half Romany named Julio Martinez, the gang provided protection for the small stores and shops that filled the neighborhood. The charge for this service was relatively low, not like the Mob, and it worked. The crime rate was low, kids went to school, and the graffiti was more like art than tagging. No one was complaining, not even the local precinct, which, while never admitting it, relied on the gang.

The Latins were liked and respected in Alphabet City not only because they kept crime down, but also because they helped people. If a guy was down on his luck, The Latins would slip him a few bucks. If a kid were acting up, The Latins would come by the family's place and take him to a gang meeting. Usually, he came back with a different attitude and the fear of God.

The Latins were big on education and on religion. They may have been tough-assed-mother-fuckers, but they were intense on learning and the church, especially the church. Every Sunday they paraded to Mass. Dressed in their leather-best with their women looking like whores and their kids like choirboys and angels. They would take up half the seats at St. Jerome's ten o'clock service, the mass that regularly produced the best collection of the weekend.

After church, weather permitting, The Latins sauntered over to Tompkins Square Park where they'd hang out for most of the day. Their music was loud, their language was profane, there was drinking and drugging, the behavior was misdemeanored to the max, and they had the most fun in town.

The Latins and Jose agreed on the need to keep Alphabet City a working-class neighborhood. They didn't want those community gardens destroyed, the low-rise apartment houses toppled, or the Community Center closed. The Latins were among Jose's strongest supporters, and he saw them as an integral part of the community. In bad weather he allowed them to use the big hall that had once been the school gym for their meetings. So what if they lit up hibachis and blunts? They were his people. It was their community.

The community. La comunidad. Somos la comunidad. He means it.

In good weather, Jose occasionally showed up at the park to toss back a couple of coolers and eat a burger fresh-off one of those half-barrel hibachis braced with cinder blocks or an empanada with its tangy crispiness. Yeah, they were his people.

Maybe nationally it was different, but locally, in Alphabet City, The Latins had become respectable, even loved.

Suddenly, things had changed.

"I was scared. I don't mind saying it. The only thing missing were tanks. Hell, they even had helicopters." Jose laughed. "I gotta tell ya, it wasn't funny. I'm just—"

"Tense?" I finished for him.

"Nervous?" Helen offered.

"Nope *asustado*; I'm still scared. Not the same, not the way I was last night, but scared about what's going to happen. What the hell were they doing? It didn't make sense."

"But the cops go after gangs all the time. It never amounts to anything."

"Nah, Nick, this wasn't the cops, it was the feds. They were leading it."

"And from what I hear they were more heavy-handed than usual," Helen added.

"Heavy-handed?"

"Planting crap. Setting people up." Helen's voice filled with fury. "They arrested forty-two Latins, including Julio Martinez, along with seven of their wives.

"Fourteen of the kids were taken into *care*. That's what the city call it when they grab somebody's kids."

"What were they charged with?" I asked.

"The usual crap," Jose answered. "Drugs, possession, intent to sell. Guns. And of course that wonderful catchall, resisting arrest. Like somebody's going to resist when the Feds got guns on their kids and old ladies."

The weeks that followed were frustrating. The justice system ground at its slowest speed. Defense lawyers were unable to find their clients, who, having been moved from holding cell to holding cell, had disappeared into the labyrinth of the jail system. When cases were finally called, one or another defendant would have been mysteriously miss-transported to the wrong court. It was bald-faced institutional crap.

Some of the Legal Aid lawyers began talking about a *writ of habeas corpus*. A couple of the attorneys talked to *The Times*; one was on local television.

However reluctantly, the system slowly, creakily cooperated. Judges called cases and the necessary hearings were held. To no one's surprise, except perhaps the mayor's, most of the cases were thrown out of court.

Some of the charges just were downright comical. Two of the charges of drug possession involved prescription painkillers; both guys had scripts written at the city-run clinic at Bellevue. The doctors came dressed in their scrubs and talked about how they should be back in the emergency room. Every time the prosecutor asked a question, they brought it up.

"How often did you see Mr. Rodriquez?"

"Not as often as I'd like, but you know I work in the emergency room. We don't have enough time. I can't imagine how late I'll have to work today to catch up from being here."

"We understand your time is valuable, Doctor," the judge commented.

"Well, Your Honor, the court's time is valuable, too."

The prosecutor shuffled his feet and announced he had no further questions.

In a number of cases the planting of evidence had been so flagrant that there were witnesses. In one building, one of the feds had accidentally dropped a bag of weapons on the stairs. The guns had spilled out in front of terrified tenants. The feds simply gathered up the weapons and carried them upstairs to plant.

It never occurred to the feds that the non-Hispanic neighbors would come to court and tell the truth. Maybe they forgot they were dealing with New Yorkers. New Yorkers may get scared, but they don't get scared off.

"Yes, sir, I saw the officers bringing weapons upstairs. One of them, I'd recognize him, but he isn't in court today, dropped the bag. I was scared, real scared. All those handguns and stuff dumped out on the stairs. I pushed my wife back inside."

"So what happened, Mr. Brownlow?"

"The cops, I guess they was cops, picked up the stuff, put it back in the bag, and went upstairs."

"Was there any gunfire?"

"What? No. Just a lot of yelling. They went upstairs and then they was yelling, 'Where are the guns? Where are the guns?'"

"Who was yelling?"

"The cops, they were doing the yelling."

"How do you know it wasn't members of the gang yelling? Maybe they were yelling."

Brownlow scoffed. "You ever hear them Latins talk? They sound P.R., know what I mean, like they don't talk American. It was the cops yelling, 'Where are the guns?' I wanted to tell them they was in that bag, but I figured they'd arrest me, too. Nah, it was them."

Maybe things would have worked better if the feds or even the cops from headquarters had asked the local precinct, but the local uniforms had been carefully excluded from the entire exercise.

The whole affair would have been Keystone-Cops-laughable if so many people hadn't been locked up. In the end, only three Latins were convicted of anything.

Julio Martinez and his wife, Angelina, both went free. It took another six months to get their three kids back, not from foster homes, but from some prison-like detention center in The Bronx.

What had the kids done? Flipping the bird and yelling "*Chupa verga*."

It didn't surprise anyone when the same big-time press that had covered the invasion was nowhere to be found after the extent of official misconduct became evident. As Julio said, "There ain't no news in people like us getting' off."

Shortly after the raids, there was a shakeup at the local precinct—new commander, new cops. Patrols were increased throughout the neighborhood. Sundays the park was loaded with police. A vendetta against The Latins. The extra cops spent most of their energies on following gang members, which left an opening for some of the local thugs who'd been kept under control by the gang.

More cops and the crime rate went up. Everyone was nervous. Intimidation by the feds and city's finest at its best. I was glad to be living in Brooklyn.

Chapter 12: Peepshow

Was it a mistake to bother? Maybe love just wasn't for me. The green monster was right, but I'm not sure it mattered. Melinda would have found somebody else, maybe not right then, but eventually. That it was Mo upset me. In my sane moments I don't think either of them meant to hurt me. At other times I see it as some kind of conspiracy— they already knew each other and simply orchestrated our chance meeting at My Lady.

At least I did get to see Melinda in some of those tantalizing dainties she bought that day. She came through with my birthday present. We didn't formally break off for a week. Then, very calmly, she told me she needed a change, which, since there had never been a commitment and certainly no exclusivity, was her way of telling me to get lost.

Not kind. Not cruel. Just matter-of-fact.

It hurt like hell. I went back to Brooklyn to my shared apartment with its ratty, unintentional-antique furniture and its musty smells that no amount of air freshener could overcome. I went back to Brooklyn and bawled like a kid.

Melinda told me there was nobody else, not anybody special. I didn't believe her, so I hung around her apartment and spied.

Dumb, jealous, possessive. Nobody showed. No Mo. Nobody.

I was freaking anyway.

How could I trust my lying eyes when the green monster knew better?

Two weeks passed. Mo called. He wanted to ask Melinda out, that was if it would be all right with me.

What could I say? "We're not going out anymore."

Like you don't know.

"Oh?" A pointless pause. "What happened?"

You, you cocksucker.

"I guess she got tired of me. Melinda likes to play."

"Play?"

Are you for real?

"Around. The field. You know, nothing exclusive, nothing permanent."

"Oh. So you were pushing for …."

I was glad he left the question unfinished.

She'll do it to you, too.

After a long pause, Mo asked "So, do you mind?"

"I told you we broke up."

"I heard you, but you have feelings."

"I'm a big boy, Mo."

"So, it's okay?

"Yeah, go for it."

Don't say I didn't warn you.

"Thanks."

We hung up. Mo, presumably to call the girl I lusted and told myself I loved and me, to sit, mope, and suffer.

Jay, my gay roommate, was coming at me like a fag in a bathhouse, so I did what any sufficiently horny and frustrated guy would—I experimented. He wanted me to be the butch, and that was fine with me. I admit he gave good head; his moustache and goatee actually gave him an edge over most women. But not over Melinda. Her technique ….

Fucking Jay was okay, but the guy was lacking what I most want in a partner, a vagina. All things considered, I prefer coitus to the alternatives.

I wanted Melinda. I wanted love. If that was not to be, I'd settle for sex.

Unhappy, frustrated, horny, and angry, I started going to peep shows, lots of peep shows. Perhaps Mrs. Kantor, the high school Freud, had been right. There was something wonderfully dirty in the watching, perhaps because I knew other men were watching and beating their meat, too. Some of the women were disturbingly attractive, especially the ones who looked hard-used, their faces worn and creased, their movements just a second off beat. I fantasized lives for them and gave them names out of my personal pathology.

One of my favorites I called *Lard-Ass*. Obviously not her performance name, which was some dumb, Frenchified nonsense. She wasn't particularly attractive. Her big ass drooped, so did the rest of her. Despite her makeup, her upper lip evidenced a mustache. Still, there was something, something that made her strangely attractive, something that spoke of warmth and caring.

I imagined her an entire slow descent of a career: a lap dancer in New Orleans, a headline stripper, one of those poor souls pulling off their clothes in places like Lewiston, Maine, and Des Moines, Iowa, now a peek show pathetic, and eventually a pro working Times Square or Ninth Avenue and being hauled in by the gendarmes.

I wanted to rescue her, just as I had wanted to rescue my mother from her histrionic madness. I hadn't been able to rescue Mom, and I knew that I couldn't rescue *Lard-Ass*. That didn't stop the fantasies.

Distrust, jealousy, obsessions. How far from Mom have I landed in the family psycho tree?

I took to waiting by the back door of the Sex Palace where Lard-Ass worked. I hoped I'd meet her coming out. Just by chance — manufactured chance. My plan: ask her for a date, which would no doubt blow her mind. No mater how scruffy I had become, I figured I was better than whatever had crawled into her life before me. Sure it was dangerous hanging around in an alley, but that just made it more tempting.

I didn't get mugged, which surprised me. And, I did get to meet her, sort of. She was leaving with a couple of the other dancers. I tried to say something to her. A bouncer, whom I hadn't seen standing near the door, grabbed me and dragged me out to the street. "No freebies," he pushed me on my way.

"I just wanted …" I called to his retreating back and realized there was no point. It was a fantasy that would never happen.

I was standing there when the three women exited the alley. They turned the other way and walked off. I was tempted to follow when I saw the bouncer lurking by the alley entrance, no doubt waiting for me to be stupid.

The whore I ended up with that night was in worse shape than Lard-Ass. Angel was everything that self-righteous moralists preach about when they condemn prostitution. A runaway from a hellish family life, she learned to turn tricks when she was fourteen. Now, at twenty-four, she was used-up and drug-addicted. It was only a matter of time before the needle killed her, so she didn't give a damn about what AIDS or some other scourge might do. Her preference was no condoms; there's nothing like a death wish. I didn't have any great urge to die, especially not as a victim of the slow-wasting epidemic that's been sweeping the world. Besides, I always have the memory of Delores and Itchy Balls. So I carry condoms.

"An extra five bucks to use a condom?" Angel demanded.

That should have been a warning.

Fuck her.

I saved my money. I wasn't going to pay for the privilege of protecting myself. That was a mistake. Actually, the whole thing was a mistake.

Angel was good, which didn't stop her from being loaded with crabs. When the itching got too bad, I went to a clinic. No big charge, but between their sliding scale and the meds, I had to skip lunch for a week. Since I only have coffee and a cigarette for breakfast, it looked to be a long, hungry week.

They were doing AIDS testing for free. Just in case, I had them draw blood. A week later I learned that so far I had dodged that nasty bullet.

Fuck it. Maybe I should just give up on women.

An idea I knew I would never follow.

Chapter 13: The Crabs of the Earth

There's something to be learned from crabs, something besides the obvious health education stuff about hygiene.

Crabs scurry about looking for food, shelter, and sex just like people. Then along comes global warming or a dose of toxic powder and poof the little buggers are toast.

I thought about the ephemeral quality of life and what it was all about. I didn't reach any conclusions. I was too busy with my own scurrying.

While I was still itching away, Frank called. I met him at Sahib Palace with enough money to pay for beer and food. I had given in to hunger and called Dad. As always, he bailed me out with a couple hundred bucks and a shit-load of guilt. The money way more than made up for the clinic and medication so I was feeling flush, as flush as a guy could feel when his car is a permanent resident of the city's impound lot and Goodwill wouldn't take his clothes, not even to use as rags.

Heading towards Queens, I figured I'd even spring for an order of *samosas*.

We can split them. That should make Frank happy.

Frank was nursing a Diet Coke, which was really out of character. It should have been a warning.

"What the hell have you gotten me into?" he rasped as soon as I sat down.

I gestured to Mahatma, but Frank signaled him not to come.

"What's the matter?"

"Hunter," he growled not looking up. "Hunter's the damn matter. That son-of-a-bitch you asked me to look up."

He took a swig of soda and banged the can down. Suddenly, he looked up directly and angrily into my eyes. "Have you got any idea …" he started.

Perhaps it was my, "Huh?" Or my mouth dropping open. He must have realized I had no clue. He stopped talking and just glared.

"Who is he?" I whispered.

"Somebody," he shot back.

"Of course he's somebody, but who?"

"Somebody with connections."

"In City Hall?"

"Beyond City Hall, beyond Albany, try Washington, fucking Washington, D.C."

"What the hell?"

"He has no history, no record, nada. The only thing I found was my way to some computer in Washington. The trail stopped dead with your basic 'need to know only' screen.

"Next day I get called into the captain's office. There are a couple of biggies from downtown. They want to know why I'm messing with the feds. I tell them I had heard some guy was involved in the local drug scene and tried to learn more about him. I guess they bought it. Just told me to forget it … him … and to keep the hell away. I'm sure they're watching."

Another slurp of soda.

"Shit."

"Jesus," I muttered. "Look, I … sorry, man. I had no idea." My throat felt raw, my hands were clammy, my voice hoarse.

"Yeah. Well, stay the fuck away from me for a while, huh. Just in case."

"Sure. Look, Frank, I really am sorry."

"You already said that. Just stay away." He turned back to his Coke. I got up. I had gone two steps when he hissed after me. "Nick."

"Yeah?"

"Be careful. Be real careful."

I headed to the office. I had more of Emily's crap stories to write, and I wanted someplace to do some hard thinking. I was feeling a lot like one of those crabs just waiting for the toxic cloud to erase me from the scrotum hair of the universe.

Chapter 14: *La Voz de Dios*

We backpacked the Inca Trail, a trek that inspired almost as much as it exhausted. Even with our mini training hikes, keeping up with my Israeli friends extended exhaustion into torture. They half-trotted up the never-ending slope. It was all I could do to keep moving.

Now and then they would stop, get the primus stove working, and brew máte. They loaded the dark liquid with sugar and ate sweet biscuits with it.

The stops gave me a shot at catching up. I would get to their stopping spot just in time to slurp and chew my share. God, I needed that caffeine and the sugar. Then off they'd go again, the five of them in that endless half-trot of the physically fit. Meanwhile, I struggled against gravity and weariness and tottered after.

Only Mo showed obvious concern for my survival. At one point he tried to take some of the stuff out of my pack and put it in his own. I wanted to let him, but I knew I couldn't.

"How do you think that would make me feel?" I gasped the question and tried to stay upright.

Mo laughed gently. "Don't be silly, Nick."

"Hey, it's a question of pride."

"There won't be much pride left when they have to helicopter you to intensive care." Then to rub it in, he added, "I wonder how you'll look in one of the local hospital's gowns."

Fuck you. I would rather drop dead then let you carry my stuff.

"I can do it," I responded as adamantly as I could gasp and held my backpack closed.

Pride is a fool's goad and a wise man's humor.

By the time we reached Machu Picchu, I was ready for that hospital bed. The Israelis were ready to search every nook and cranny. I hated them, Peru, and especially myself.

Come the next afternoon, I convinced myself I was sufficiently rested and ready to go exploring. Recuperation comes easily to the young. It doesn't last long for those who have taken lousy care of themselves. I was moving, barely, without energy or enthusiasm.

Given the darkness of my mood, there were way too many tourists snapping photos in the more popular spots. I looked for a less-used path and followed it. It led to a small plaza, pretty enough, but with no grand vistas or elaborate stonework. I found a comfortable place to sit and plopped myself down to watch the slow play of shadows on the ancient walls. Even though I was feeling better, I just wanted to sit. I just wanted to be alone.

I studied the vines growing on the stone walls. It seemed like man and nature had fought a long battle and finally reached a precarious truce.

I was so preoccupied with my musings that I didn't notice the old man with his wide-brimmed hat and brightly colored, llama wool poncho. It was only when he started to play his pan flute that I realized he was there, squatting against one of the walls of the plaza. His hat, with a bright orange band, lay on the ground next to him.

The design on his poncho upset me. A crimson serpent wound itself around a central yellow figure: its prey. That prey could have been a monkey or it could have been a person. Perhaps me.

The old guy played long, sweet, echoing songs I didn't recognize. I was mesmerized by the music and by his shadow, which seemed to lengthen with the pull of his melodies.

It must have been some time before I became conscious that they had gathered. At first a knot of people and then a good sized crowd. Laborers, men and women, finished with their day's work, gathered in silent appreciation of the musician's artistry.

One of them spoke in a low tone. "*La voz de Dios.*" The words were repeated in a gathering murmur. "*La voz de Dios.*" "*La voz de Dios.*"

The voice of God, what the hell does that mean?

The old man slipped away. The voices faded. I was again alone.

What the hell just happened?

Mo was standing over me. He had wet a handkerchief with his canteen and was using it to mop my face.

"Hey, Nick, wake up, man."

I shivered with the cold of fatigue and fever.

He held the canteen to my lips. I managed a swallow, followed by a gulp.

"Easy, easy." Mo helped me to my feet. He supported me as we wobbled back to our campsite. For two days he nursed me. The others gave occasional help, but it was Mo who really took care.

When I felt strong enough to sit up and talk, I told Mo about the old man. He thought for a moment and then spoke very softly. His voice was somehow different; it had the timbre of authority. "It is a great responsibility to have heard the voice of God."

"What do you—"

He put his finger to his lips. "It is," Mo repeated with even deeper emphasis, "a great responsibility."

"The voice of God," I thought as I let myself fall back to sleep. "*La voz de Dios.* What will the fucking responsibility be?"

Chapter 15: A Friend in Need

I resented Mo's mothering. At the same time, I loved him for his gentle concern. Of the five Israelis, his was the only friendship I wanted. By the time we were back in Lima, I was convinced that we should, and would, keep the lines of communication open. He gave me his email address and said it was the best way of staying in touch.

Resolutions are wonderful things. You make them with the best of intentions and break them with the easiest of excuses.

During the rest of my stay in South America, I emailed Mo twice from the pensione. I got back noncommittal replies, no mention of where he was or what he was doing. Instead of personal information, he sent photographs of Peru: scenery, natives, even a few of me, beautiful shots, but not one picture of Mo or the others. Not of the jeeps. Not even of the camping gear. There were a few tourists, people I hadn't met and never would, but not a sign of my five companions.

When I got back to New York I had a new email account. But by then I had made the necessary excuses to myself, and Mo had been pushed to the back of my mind. When he came up to me on a Manhattan street, it seemed like some small miracle. When he started seeing Melinda, it seemed more like a tiny cosmic joke with me as the brunt.

I was angry, but Mo, with his *Mossad* connections, might still have his uses.

Frank had not found out anything about Hunter other than he was connected to the feds. There was no way my cop friend was willing to risk making them angry just to do me a favor. But Mo was different. Not only did he work for another country's government, and in their most clandestine department, but also he owed me. At least in my mind he owed me and big. In the currency of reciprocity, Melinda certainly carried a big price.

It was late when I called. I was too hopped up to think about time. If I had, I probably would have called anyway.

Either he's going to help me or he's not. Either he knows he owes me of he doesn't. Either he's going to help me get that Pulitzer or …

It wasn't the kind of thinking that waits. Three in the morning I called.

After he fumbled himself to wakefulness, Mo demanded, "What the devil do you think you're doing calling me in the middle of the night?"

"Sorry." I tried to mean it.

There was a moment of silence.

"This better be important."

"It is." Suddenly I felt less sure. "Can we get together tomorrow morning?"

"It is tomorrow morning."

"Yeah, sorry about that. Can we get together this morning?"

"Now?"

"No. Not now. How about breakfast? My treat."

"A doughnut and coffee isn't my idea of breakfast."

"A real breakfast. Eggs. Even bacon if you want."

I can be sarcastic, too.

"Cute."

"Yeah. Sorry … so, can we meet?"

"Yeah. Sure. Okay." He named a coffee shop in the financial district.

"You want to travel all that way?" I was trying to be snide. I assumed that he was sleeping at Melinda's.

"I live nearby."

My God, a personal detail. What the hell, push it.

"Why don't we just meet up at your place?"

"Maybe some other time." His voice strained. "It wouldn't be a good idea this morning."

"Why? Did I wake somebody else up?" Jealousy puked its head back into my thoughts.

"It just wouldn't. Okay?"

I backed off. "Yeah, I'll see you at the coffee shop. What time?"

"Nine. No make it nine thirty."

I was there at quarter-to. The place was cleaner than the joints I usually frequented, cleaner and pricier. I could see empty booths toward the back. No matter, a surly waiter with a bow tie, which bounced on his large Adam's apple, and a stained white shirt, told me I'd have to wait for a table. He kept offering me a stool at the counter.

Each time I explained I was meeting somebody, that he was due at nine thirty, and that we would need a table where we could talk. Finally, he gave up with a shrug and said a table might come available toward the rear of the restaurant. I told him that would be perfect and waited some more.

I stood by the door and watched the busy day of the financial district come to life in a tide of coffee, Danish, well-dressed men, and attractive women. Nine twenty-five I was seated, a cup of over-priced coffee on the way.

Nine thirty exactly, Mo entered the restaurant. He acted as if he didn't see me.

I waved.

"Put your arm down," the same waiter hissed at me. "Put your arm down. He'll get to you."

"How do you …" The man was already moving away.

"Hey, Nick, what are you doing here?" Mo acted as if it were a totally chance encounter.

I rose to the occasion. "I have a meeting at the Trade Center."

"I hope they're not expecting formal."

"Hey, I am who I am. If they want to talk with me, they will no matter how I dress."

Lame.

I looked at my reflection in the wide mirrored rail that served as a splash-back for the table. Besides needing a haircut and a shave, I was dressed in a plaid flannel shirt that had seen many better days. I couldn't see my jeans, but I knew they were equally disreputable. I looked like a castoff version of Jose.

For the first time, I thought about how the other customers were dressed. Businessmen and women, they must have wondered what a bum like me was doing there.

"Mind if I sit down?" Mo had to repeat the question before I caught myself and gestured toward the bench opposite me.

The banquettes had high backs with heavy glass partitions on top, which gave much more privacy than most coffee shops. Given the waiter's behavior, I wondered if the restaurant was *Mossad* run. Before

I could say something that probably would have been as stupid as my clothes, the waiter came over and asked Mo if he wanted coffee.

"And my usual breakfast."

"Yes, Sir." He turned to me. "What would you like?"

I noticed a condescending change in his voice and the absence of the *sir*.

"A cheese omelet, an English muffin, orange juice, and hash browns." It was the first real breakfast that came to my mind.

"What size orange juice?"

"Large." I tried to put some sarcasm in my voice as if he had been dumb to ask. He nodded curtly and turned away. As soon as he did, I felt like a jerk. I had blown a wad on a breakfast that I really didn't want just to let some stupid waiter know I was somebody, like it really makes you somebody to have breakfast in a coffee shop.

"You must be hungry," Mo observed. "Pulling an all-nighter will do that to you," he added in the first kindly tone he had used since I awakened him.

Not knowing what else to do, I laughed.

"Yeah, famished." I felt closer to him, less angry, now that we were together. For one thing, I could see the concern in his eyes.

"Have you been losing weight?"

I hadn't thought about it before, but yeah, I was. My clothes had become looser and I was using one notch tighter on my belt.

"Working too much," I mumbled.

Keep your mouth shut about her. Just act normal.

The corners of Mo's mouth twitched. I figured he wanted to say something, or maybe I just wanted him to want to say something. Either way, whatever it was, I was sure I didn't want to hear it, not anything about her.

I launched right into it. "There's this guy I need to find out about."

Chapter 16: Dinner with Jose

Jose had two wives. There was his office wife Helen, his secretary. She not only handled the office but also managed the dingy studio that served as Jose's legal home: making sure it was clean, that his clothes were washed, that there was food, even buying his cigarillos.

Technically, Jose was forced to reside in Alphabet City. The rules were simple: The principle officer of a community center that used free city accommodations had to live in the community. His studio was near the Center in a building that could and should be condemned.

"I gotta tell ya, some nights I come home and it's like a tornado. I keep wondering if it will fall down before they knock it down."

"Like the place I was living."

"Yeah, *Muchacho*, but I can't run away to Brooklyn or home to Queens. I gotta stay and fight."

Jose's real wife, the one to whom he was truly devoted and on whom he would never cheat, was a big-breasted Puerto Rican beauty. They had met when he was a young man, a college student. He was visiting his grandparents who still lived on the island. Older than Jose, Maria had already been married and divorced. Despite the difference in their ages, it had been love from the first.

Maria lived in an apartment in the projects in Queens. That was where they lived during Jose's student years, and she had never left. To Maria it was home, and the people around her were family.

The newspaper for which I worked covered that part of Queens. That was the only reason Jose had broken his usual rule and invited me for supper. Generally, their relationship was kept as private as possible. People connected to the Center weren't allowed anywhere near Maria. She never attended events at the Center. Never came to the meetings. As far as I could tell, only Helen and Jose's old friend and partner, David, had ever met Maria. Not only did this policy protect Maria from the constant crises at the Center, but it also helped maintain that legally necessary fiction that she and Jose were separated, that he lived in Alphabet City and she in Queens.

That was the story for public consumption. Jose and Maria were separated. That quasi-lie allowed Maria to keep their wonderfully low-rent apartment, which was now in her name. Whatever the official story, everybody at the Center and everybody who lived near them in Queens knew how dedicated Jose was to *la reina de mi vida*.

Weeknights, Jose worked late. Exhausted, he would go to that cruddy studio where he'd nuke the supper Helen had arranged and fall into his lonely bed. Workweeks were isolated and difficult times.

Jose's weekends were another thing entirely with at least one day, preferably two, spent together with his *reina* in their apartment. There they could fall into what Helen called, "the quiet domesticity of the happily married."

When she heard that I was going to meet Maria, Helen felt compelled to fill me in.

"Let's go get a cup of coffee," she suggested, her tone made it more of a demand.

We bought a couple of cups and sat on a graffiti-scarred bench outside the coffee shop. What an odd couple we must have seemed to passersby, Helen with her off-the-page-of-the-latest-magazine clothes, and me scruffy and poor.

Helen talked about Jose and Maria. "Once in a great while, they break routine and have a friend to dinner, or they go out to a restaurant, or very rarely to a movie. But most of their nights together are like clockwork.

"Maria cooks, usually something traditional, a recipe she learned growing up in Ponce. They eat at the kitchen table, almost always by candlelight. Maria thinks it's romantic. Jose says it makes him think Con Ed has shut off the power.

"There are flowers. He always buys them from the same kiosk at the Times Square Subway station. When he's changing trains, he buys her flowers. She loves them, especially roses, red roses. No matter what he has to do without, he brings her those roses.

"Then, while Maria does the dishes, Jose goes for a short walk and a smoke. Smoking is one of the few things they disagree about. And it's probably the only one where Maria makes the rule. No matter what the weather, Jose has to go outside to have his smokes, and you know he has to smoke those damn things.

"By the time Jose finishes one of those little cigars of his, Maria has the dishes finished. Then they settle in to watch television. A simple routine. A Momma and Papa thing. That's life."

It seemed both strange and understandable that Jose, who was always racing around juggling crises, meetings, court appearances, and endlessly talking, needed such a haven of quiet habit.

"No worries," I told Helen; "it's just for dinner. Nothing to upset her. Just friendly."

"Just remember, you upset Jose and you upset everyone at the Center."

I understood.

I wore my best clothes and brought flowers—a bouquet, no roses.

Jose welcomed me with an embrace. While Maria put the flowers in water, Jose invited me to sit.

The deep-green brocade of the couch was well worn from hundreds of nights of simple domesticity. Photographs of family and scenes from Puerto Rico hung on the walls. There, too, were Jose's diplomas and certificates.

When I remarked on them, how many there were, Jose responded, "Maria likes to have them. I gotta tell ya, I could care less."

"Jose's a compulsive news-watcher," Helen had continued. "He goes back outside for another smoke at ten thirty. That way he's finished before the major network news comes on."

Maria adored Jose. She spent the entire evening just watching him, drinking him in, waiting on him, trying to anticipate his needs and wants.

Jose's love seemed more understated, but he never let a chance to kiss his wife, pat her, or in some other way show his affection, pass. There was a synchronization of body language: the way they crossed and uncrossed their legs at the same moment, the way they seemed to pick up their coffee cups at the same instant. Even the rhythm of their words was the same. It was a union of souls.

Jose had no children. Maria had two from her previous marriage, a son and a daughter. The daughter was married by the time that Maria had met Jose. There were three grandchildren from that marriage. The children's photographs were distinguished by the same sweet, loving smile and flashing eyes that I saw in Maria.

Although she and Jose tried to entice them to come to New York, Maria's daughter and son-in-law had opted to stay in Ponce, where they both worked in hotels. Maria made no secret of how badly she missed her *nietos*.

Maria's son had lived with Jose and Maria during the early years of their marriage. He still lived in Queens, but they seldom saw him anymore. Unmarried, he was a source of anxiety, especially for Maria. Miguel wasn't a druggie or a drinker, but he was a womanizer, and he didn't like the idea of work, so he drifted from job to job. The way Helen described him, he sounded a lot like me except for being more successful with the ladies.

"I worry about him," Maria said while Jose stroked her back.

I had been asking about the many photographs hung on walls and set on tables and bookcases.

Does my dad have the same concerns about his younger son?

I felt guilty at that thought; I also felt good. Watching the loving couple before me, it seemed the concern and love of parents was a good thing to have even if it did mean anxiety and grief for them.

It was a crisp Saturday evening when I had been their dinner guest. Maria made *alcapurrias carne, arroz con gandules*, and, for a sweet ending, flan. It was delicious. I loved it, and I loved the marriage I saw before me, a marriage totally different from my parents',one built on warmth and caring. For the first time I could remember, I thought about someday finding someone, someone special, someone forever, someone with whom I could savor life.

Will I ever find her?

Probably not.

Not Marcie or Melinda.

I wish.

Estrella flashed through my mind.

"How do you take it?" Maria was asking about my coffee.

"Black, lots of sugar," Jose answered for me.

"*Iqual gue tu, guerido.*" She spooned sugar into two cups.

After coffee, Jose and I went out for a smoke. We took his usual route through the project. He waved to some folks; they waved back.

Despite my promise to Helen, we talked about the Center. Things weren't looking good. The city had given John Hunter the deed to the building, and he sent a certified letter saying the Center had until the end of the month to vacate. David was looking for alternative spaces, possibly a vacant storefront that might be donated, while Jose closeted himself with the lawyers and tried to come up with new strategies.

"I gotta tell ya, I never knew there were so many loopholes in the universe," Jose offered.

"Have you found one?"

"Nope, not yet, but we're looking."

"What do you think will happen?"

"The end of the month will come. I'll stand in the doorway defying them like a P.R. Lester Maddox. The news will cover it, so Hunter will probably back off for a while—a little while, but it'll buy us some time. For whatever reason he's real private, doesn't want anybody knowing anything about him."

"A bit more than that." I filled Jose in on my request to Frank. I added that I had another possible source, but nothing about Mo or the *Mossad*. Some things just need to be kept secret. I figured that Mo, playing the boyfriend, must have stopped by the center at least once to pick Melinda up for lunch or at the end of her work.

Maybe he dropped her off one morning after he'd spent the night?

I imagined my buddy in Melinda's bed and felt the gorge of jealousy rising.

Still, no way I wanted Jose or Melinda to have any suspicions about Mo's connections.

"I appreciate it," Jose said, "but be careful. There are some pretty nasty guys involved in this."

Like I don't already know.

"Tell me about it. Burmaste for one." It was the first time I had mentioned the politico to Jose. I wanted to see his reaction.

"That son of a bitch. I'd like to see him in hell."

"That bad, huh?"

"He'd murder his own mother for a nickel. A real hatchet man."

"A well-connected hatchet man."

Jose punched his right hand into his left. "That bastard sold out the Hispanic community to sit on the right hand of a mayor who's all about greed." He started walking back to the building entrance. Suddenly, he stopped and whirled around to look at me.

"Have you seen his club building?"

I nodded.

I had gone by it one day and been taken aback. In the middle of Alphabet City's urban decay, there it sat, a squat pillbox of a building looking as if it could withstand not just a wrecking ball but a military assault. A fortress with a few small windows. A place unwelcoming to all.

"Can you imagine how many people you have to screw to feel you need a bunker like that?" Jose shook his head solemnly.

I laughed. "On the other hand, he has all that protection while you walk around like this." I made a gesture to take in the scene.

"I told you, Julio and The Latins have my back."

"Martinez and his gang? Shit, man, can they even cover their own backs? Look how the cops are all over them."

Jose shot me a withering look. "Well, I'm not gonna worry about it, and don't you go upsetting Maria … or Helen either. Understand?"

"Yeah, I understand; but I wish—"

Jose wheeled away from me and walked toward the building entrance. He hit the buzzer three times in rapid succession, and Maria buzzed us in. In the elevator he turned to me and harshly whispered, "Not a word."

"I understand, man." I understood and I worried. I worried about Jose. I worried about the Center. I worried about the other people I had gotten to know and like and, to be honest, I worried about me.

Chapter 17: Washington

The cherry blossoms were definitely not in bloom.

Most people think of Washington, D.C. as a place of cherry blossoms, monuments, great white buildings, and consequential decisions. For me it will always be as I experienced it then, shrouded in damp snow and grayness. A day to devour body and soul.

In my memory, Washington is filled with unplowed roads winding through an uncharted wilderness of suburban homes. It is a place of shadowy intrigue, the sole purpose of which is to concentrate wealth and power in the hands of the few.

I didn't always feel that way. In sixth grade we took a class trip to the nation's capital. It was springtime and beautiful. Our buses rolled past those monuments as teachers told us about the heroes of history. We visited Congress and the White House. Will and I ran up and down the stairs of the Lincoln Memorial and then the Washington Monument. At night the two of us, high on exhaustion, snuck out of our room and rode the elevators with the other kids. Then, a bunch of us, boys and girls, piled into one room where we giggled and talked until dawn. Washington was a city of freedom, a place of liberty.

That had been my age of innocence. Now, I know better, or should I say worse.

John Hunter didn't exist. That had been Mo's conclusion. The thin, owl-eyed man whom I had met at Jose's office was no more John Hunter than I was. Somewhere between Langley, Virginia, and New York City, someone had created a being from the fabric of computers, government connections, and wealth. The assets Hunter appeared to own were traced to a privately owned corporation located at an address near Bethesda, Maryland. Mo gave me money for plane fare and expenses and the use of a credit card so I could rent a car, sleep in a motel, and otherwise stay alive while I tried to find out more about that corporation.

I wasn't sure why Mo wanted to give me so much help. It certainly went beyond guilt over Melinda or bonds formed while hiking in Peru. I figured there was a *Mossad* connection, something to do with his mission in the States. What that mission was I had no clue, but that's what investigative reporting is about, skating on the edge of the world's secrets until finding out what they are or falling through the ice. One thing was sure: Mr. Pulitzer was waiting for me somewhere across that not-too-frozen pond, waiting to see how well I could skate.

The address Mo gave me turned out to be not an office building, but a house. It would have blended in with its suburban neighbors—just another upper-level government worker's commuter home—except for the high cinderblock wall and the tidy white gatehouse with its armed guard just inside the sliding metal fence.

Cars splashed through the slush as they came and went. The snow picked up; the wind whirled thick flakes around me. I parked half a block away. With a pair of binoculars borrowed from a roommate, I could watch without being too conspicuous. I used the camera Dad had given me when I was a naive make-believe student in Chile and photographed the comings and goings. As Mo had instructed, I made notes of license plates, times, numbers of passengers, and general appearance of vehicles.

They were a suspicious lot. Most of the windows heavily tinted, the cars crawled up the street, some circling the block before pulling up to the gate.

Every few hours I, too, drove around the block and then returned, each time parking in a different spot. It was my idea of being a private eye.

I hoped my pathetic subterfuge was working. Not sure I was getting any useful information, I sat for hours.

At 3:20, three men came out of the gate and walked down the street. The sidewalks were impassable, so they trudged in the gutter. Hunched against the weather, the three were in heated discussion, gesticulating and often stopping as they discussed some point or other. At first, I figured they were taking a smoke break, but they didn't light up. Given the horrible weather, there had to be a reason for them being outside.

Wish I could hear. This has to be something top secret.

They were a strange trio. One looked to be an Arab. He wore an Arab headdress, which I later learned was called a *kufia,* and was dressed in a dark wool robe. Later on Mo taught me the name for that, too, a *dishdashah*. He kept his arms wrapped around himself. I figured that robe wasn't keeping out the wintery March weather.

The second guy was a fair-skinned, white guy in an expensive overcoat. He wasn't wearing a hat and kept brushing the snow out of his hair. Every few moments, he'd look down at his feet and stomp.

Guess he doesn't like snow on his shoes.

The third man was bulkier than the others, with a dark complexion. Him I recognized. It was Burmaste, the shadowy Cuban who wielded so much political clout with New York's mayor.

What the hell is he doing here?

I snapped picture after picture until they turned back into the driveway.

I hope Mo can figure this out.

It was late, and the snow was piling. I figured on heading back to the airport. Just then a tan Chevy with government plates came out of the gate. I took a picture, jotted down the plate number, and checked the time. It was 4:30, quitting time for office workers.

Shit, I bet he works here. Who is he? If I follow him home, I can get a name, a real name. Then Mo can find out what department.

When the car turned a corner, I pulled a fast U-turn and followed.

It was a difficult slipping and sliding drive. There were few other cars on the road. The weather had worsened; many people must have already sought the warm safety of their homes. Tailing someone in the snow seemed like the height of folly. I expected at any moment a goon squad would appear from nowhere and rough me up or even kill me.

When life sends us a mechanical rabbit to chase, what reporter doesn't let out a howl and take up the race?

The Chevy pulled up at a Seven-Eleven. The driver, dressed in a tan overcoat, wearing leather gloves and a homburg, walked toward the pay phone attached to the store's outside wall.

Shit, he's calling for reinforcements.

My tongue thickened with fear, my hands felt sweaty despite the freezing temperatures and I was ready to get the hell out of there.

He walked passed the phone and into the store. I gulped air with relief.

A couple minutes later, he came out with a cup of coffee, stopped to take a sip, and got back into his car.

Boy, I wanted a cup of joe, too. I settled for rolling down my window and snapping another picture of the guy.

He backed out of his spot and returned to the road. I waited a moment for him to get clear and swung in behind.

The snow was getting heavier. The wipers struggled to keep up. The defroster was set at its highest level, and I was sweating a clammy, uncomfortable perspiration that mixed heat, fear, effort, and exhaustion. I wondered how long I could keep following. A siren broke my concentration.

The Maryland state trooper who stopped me was exceedingly polite. There had been a report of a hit-and-run. The description matched my car; would I mind showing him some identification. He checked the car as if he was looking for evidence of an accident. Finding none, he sent me on my way with a warning to be careful.

"The roads are bad. Looks like it'll be getting worse. You might want to look for a motel, sir."

I acknowledged his warning and started the motor. The Chevy was long gone. I was uncomfortable and hungry and hadn't the slightest idea where I was.

I picked a direction and drove until I got to a main road, one that appeared on the lousy map the rental company had given me and, better yet, had been plowed.

I found a diner and stopped for food and caffeine. I was eating the last of my pasty blueberry pie when the obvious hit me.

There was no fucking way somebody could have described a car or that a policeman could have recognized one from a description, not in this storm.

I went to the pay phone, called Mo's cell, and told him my cover had been blown.

"You'd better get back here."

"Okay, I have an open-ended plane ticket. I can grab the next Delta flight."

"Not from what I'm hearing. The planes won't be flying, not in this weather."

"What?"

"Snow, man. The planes are probably grounded already."

"Oh, yeah. So, what should I do?"

"Stay safe."

Not much help there. You're the fucking spy.

"What about Amtrak? Will it be running?" I asked.

"Who knows? Try it. I'm sure you'll hit delays. Like I said, 'Try to stay safe.'"

I expected Mo to somehow magically have answers. He offered none.

"This is beginning to sound like a Hitchcock movie," I said.

"Welcome to my world."

Terror shivered inside.

The connection went dead.

Chapter 18: Train Ride

I loved snow as a little kid. Not just the days off from school and the occasional ski trips with Dad. Not even the freewheeling joy of snowball fights and the sometimes chance to push snow in Sue Tremont's pretty, freckled face. It was the sense of renewal. Snow made the entire world over.

At the end of a long day of shoveling, throwing snowballs, and freedom from school, the family gathered around our fireplace with its crackling wood and dancing flames. We drank mugs of hot chocolate with little marshmallows. I would feel like my soul had been lightened and that the world could not get better. I'd cuddle next to Mom and sip my cocoa.

Those times, I even loved my brother Jim. I loved him even though that same afternoon he had pelted me with snowballs, even though he had dumped a shovel of snow on my head, even though he called me shrimp and peewee, even though I knew the next day he'd tell the kids in school that I had cried when he had washed my face with the cold, stinging snow.

After the fire died, I'd go up to my room, snuggle under the thick down red and blue quilt, wait for Mom to come kiss me goodnight. After she turned out the lights, I'd pat my dog's muzzle until I drifted off to dreams that always seemed to end as happily as the day.

Looking back, those snowy days in the years before my parents' divorce seem idyllic. By contrast, the Amtrak trip from Washington to New York was a journey through hell.

Departures were delayed. I wandered through the dampness of the food court. The smell of franchised burgers, cloyingly sweet cinnamon buns, Chinese food, and pizza converged to remind me of my hunger. I was even more tired than hungry. I wanted to pass out at one of the tables.

To tired for food, I bought a super-sized cup of coffee loaded with sugar and a newspaper. I read about the latest scandals and accusations that serve as entertainment inside the Washington beltway.

The loudspeaker voice crackled and droned, repeating itself over and over. "We are exper … encing … unexpec … delays."

People, most of them looking as harried as I felt, pushed and shoved their way about.

Again the announcement, "We are exper … encing … unexpec … delays."

I found my way to the men's room. It smelled of piss and the air was foul with the smell of somebody's recent bowel movement. The tinny sound of the loudspeaker followed. "We are exper … encing … unexpec … delays."

I stood at a urinal and feeling my shoes sticking to the floor, tried to relieve myself. As is so often the case in public bathrooms, I had trouble getting started.

Eventually, the staticky, disembodied voice announced the train to New York was ready to board. A fast-moving flood of people moved toward Gate Six. I thought of stopping to buy something to eat, a soda, and maybe something other than that newspaper to read. I decided getting a good seat was more important. If I remembered trains correctly, there would be a dining car and vendors selling newspapers and magazines.

It was a game of musical chairs. When the jostling stopped, there were few empty seats. I ended up standing next to a portly man in an ill-fitting green suit. His wire-rimmed glasses were incongruous given his large red drinker's nose. His briefcase, battered and scarred, rested on the seat next to him.

This guy should be in the circus.

"Do you mind?" I gestured towards the seat.

"Yeah, sure." His breath carried the clear odor of alcohol. He moved the briefcase onto his lap, dropped his double chin onto his breast, and was snoring before I could squeeze by his knees and into my seat.

There were three unused frames on the roll of film in my camera. I snapped a couple pictures of the guy.

The train was overheated. I was thankful we were leaving late. Most of the passengers had been sitting around long enough for snow to melt and clothes to dry. Even still, the car steamed.

The train jerked underway and almost immediately staggered to a stop. For three hours we lurched our way north toward Baltimore. Passengers grumbled. A few said they should have waited for the weather to clear and taken the shuttle as they usually did.

The man next to me said nothing. He just snored louder.

A conductor threaded his way though the crowded car. I asked him about the dining car.

He laughed. "If we had one, which we don't, it would be so full by now you'd have to wait 'till New York to get into it."

"No food? How about coffee?"

"Nah. When we get to Baltimore, there'll be some vendors coming onboard. Their stuff isn't any good, and they charge three times what it's worth, but it'll keep you from dying of hunger. The coffee is usually okay, overpriced, too, but okay. The thing is they're going to be so mobbed you'd better watch for them and try to get to a door where you see they're going to come onboard."

"That means giving up my seat?"

"Put something on it. Borrow this fella's case and put it on the seat. Usually folks respect that."

"Thanks."

He held out his hand. For a second, I was going to shake it. Then I realized what he wanted. I reached into my pocket and pulled out a dollar. Looking into his eyes, I thought better of it and reached again. I came up with a five. He flashed me a smile, pocketed the bill and started to move off.

I grabbed my camera and shot the last exposure on the roll.

And he says the vendors are a rip-off.

The conductor's advice came in handy, but not because I bought anything from the vendors. I ended up getting off the train in Baltimore.

As we rolled into the station, I kept my eyes on the platform watching for those peddlers. I saw something else, something that made my heart stop, and then, with a surge of adrenalin, start pumping furiously. There were police, too many for the normal run of things. They were standing in pairs. With each pair was another person dressed in a dark suit.

F.B.I. They're looking for me. I've got to get the hell off!

As nonchalantly as I could, lurching from seat to seat with the sway of the train, I made my way into the vestibule. The conductor came through opening the doors as we slowed. Remembering our conversation and his tip, he said nothing and went on his way even though I was standing on the yellow painted area with the stenciled warning, "DANGER No Standing In This Area"

Watching for a point where the crowd was reasonably thick and no police were close, I picked my spot and dropped onto the platform. I had to run a bit to keep from falling. Even at that, I stumbled.

Luckily, a guy in the crowd grabbed me as I lurched into him.

My adrenalin was working. I grabbed the guy's hand and shook it, even putting one arm around his back. In case the police were watching, I wanted them to see two friends connecting. I dragged the poor fellow along with me all the while thanking him profusely for his quick thinking and talking about my likely fall if it had not been for him.

This total stranger must have thought I was manic or high on speed, but he didn't resist, even though I was pulling him away from the train, which he may well have been planning to board.

When we got near a gate into the station proper, I pumped his hand once more with a final thanks and dodged through the gateway. Glancing back, I saw him scratch his head, check his wallet to make sure I hadn't pilfered it, shrug, and trot back towards the train.

I hope he gets a seat.

I couldn't help smiling.

Poor bugger.

I found my way to the comparative safety of a men's room. I went into one of the stalls. God, I needed to relieve myself. I also needed a place to hide.

I waited for what seemed an eternity. Men came in and out, flushing, farting, pissing, banging doors, but no police announced themselves, no cops hammered on the metal, stall doors. My heart slowed down. I could breathe again.

I left my sanctuary and walked as calmly as I could into the station proper.

Some people were standing in small knots, talking. I figured one of the groups might be gossiping about the police presence.

I sidled over to the closest group.

"I called her for a date, but she wasn't interested."

"That's too bad. I thought she'd gotten over him," a woman responded.

"Nah, she's still got the hots."

"For that loser?"

They all laughed.

I moved on to another group.

"That much? I wouldn't."

"Some guys are all about flash."

"From what I heard, that's all he's got in him."

I tried a third knot of people. I had finally hit pay dirt.

"Did they catch him?"

"I think so."

"What was he thinking of?"

"That he hated his ex. I can relate."

"Traveling by Amtrak. Boy, that guy had balls."

"More likely dumb."

"Or nuts."

"Be it'll be on the news."

"Anyone get a look at them?"

"Yeah," a short, plain woman pushed her way into the group. "I saw them. Cute kid, but the guy creeped me out. Real tall, thin, long stringy hair. Sure didn't look like that kid's father."

"A pedophile?"

"I heard it was the dad."

"Maybe it'll be on the news."

The group of them moved away. I stood in the middle of the Baltimore Station and cursed the situation.

Shit. I didn't have to get off the train at all. They were looking for someone else.

Chapter 19: Baltimore

Downtown Baltimore in the middle of a snowstorm that was bringing the East to its knees—not the place I wanted to be. I made another phone call. Mo told me to hole up.

Like I got a choice.

I found a hotel near the station, an old place, perhaps once grand but long since outmoded by Holiday Inns and Best Western and especially by Marriott and Sheraton. The ceilings were high, the chandeliers old-fashioned, once impressive but now missing many of their crystal prisms, the molding detailed in its grime, the televisions small, and room service overpriced. The maroon, gold-flecked wallpaper was dog-eared. The bathroom fixtures were discolored and cracked. The vanity mirror had worn spots that made my reflection look more blotched and sickly than it was.

Is that the real me? What I'm doomed to become?

The theme from *The Twilight Zone* played in my mind.

The hotel offered one amenity: internet access. I dropped my camera, binoculars, and the paper bag that held a change of clothes and my toothbrush in Room 315 and went back to the lobby to check emails.

There was lots of spam and two that mattered.

One was from my father, who had finally remarried and was living in sunny Florida. He and my stepmother Sylvia, whom I had only met twice, were leaving on a week's cruise.

Take care of yourself; we'll have dinner when Syl and I get back."

Sylvia and I would probably never make it past obligatory civility, but Dad loved her, and I loved him. At least they could have fun spending my inheritance.

The second email was from Marcie. That one hurt. I really didn't want to hear from her, especially while I was still mourning after Melinda. I almost hit delete. My finger wavered. I opened and read.

"I still love you," she started.

Oh, shit.

"I wish we could be together."

No, no.

"I know that I can love. Can you?"

Below the belt. I love Melinda.

"I only hope that you can find somebody."

But she's with fucking Mo.

"I wish you only happiness."

God, damn you.

My eyes teared.

God, fucking damn you.

I pictured Melinda.

I could never be good enough for her. Maybe all I deserve in life is a case of crabs.

I felt like an asshole, an itchy asshole.

I retreated to my room and jumped into the shower which drizzled lukewarm into the cracked and yellowed tub. Then I called for some overpriced room service and turned on the TV. Besides being small, it had a lousy, grainy, jumpy picture. CNN was preoccupied with what I already knew, that a blizzard was raging along the East Coast.

There was a knock. An unpleasant, older man, bits of green between his teeth, his breath smelling of garlic, wearing a decrepit uniform, which matched the hotel decor and was a size too small, arrived with my coffee and a dried-out sandwich.

"Am I supposed to pay for that?" I pointed at the purported ham and cheese on rye.

"With this weather you're lucky to get anything. I should have been home three hours ago, but they won't let me leave," the bellman whined. He held out his hand for a tip.

Intimidated, I pulled five bucks out of my pocket. I wanted to fish around for something less. Thought of giving him an I.O.U. Giving up, I handed him the five.

"Thanks"

"Yeah, welcome."

At least it's Mo's money, not mine.

I sat at the chipped, stained desk and tried to eat. The sandwich was worse than it looked. The coffee, once doctored with enough sugar, was tepid but drinkable.

I finished the coffee, pulled off my shirt and pants, peeled back the faded maroon spread, turned off the lights and television, and fell onto the bed.

Somebody had pulled one drape off a couple of its hooks and the eerie snow-filled light from the street made a pattern on the ceiling. I stared at the ceiling and tried to make the light and shadows look like something, anything.

Making sense out of nothing or nothing out of sense: is that my life's mission?

I figured I was lucky to get a hotel room at all, what with the weather. I lay on the lumpy bed and waited to fall asleep. Lying there I rehearsed my personal pity party.

Sleep did not come easily. I cursed myself for drinking the coffee, even though caffeine had never kept me awake.

Any excuse in a storm.

I tossed, turned, itched, scratched, got up and pissed, turned the TV on and then off, smoked one cigarette then another, did all the dumb things that were not going to help anyway. I was beginning to think about jacking off, always a good method to lower the internal thermostat, when the screaming started.

The hotel was old. The walls were thick and solid. Nevertheless, I could hear them going at it in the next room. Arguing about money.

She expected fifty bucks.

Now that she was in his room and ready to give him some action, he only wanted to pay thirty.

"Because you're a dirty skank," he yelled.

Something banged into the wall right behind my head.

"Fuck you!"

A second crash.

Another lamp bites the dust.

"Hey, I got to pay for that. Now, you're getting nothin', you crazy whore. Get the hell out of here or I'm calling the cops."

"Yeah, sure, and telling them what? That you had a fight with the pross you invited up? But, know what? You're right I'm out of here. You're a goddamned nut job."

"Fuck you."

Another object hit a wall.

"I can't believe Tony set me up with you."

"You can't believe? You can't believe. I ask the doorman of a respectable hotel to get me a girl and he sends me a douche bag like you. Jesus, who'd want to fuck a cunt like you anyway?"

"You would if I lowered the price. Truth is no girl would touch you for less than fifty."

"Fuck you."

"You wish. Can you even get it up?"

"Bitch!"

There was a new crash, then a thud.

The next sound was the slamming of a door in the hallway.

Curiosity, plus the sudden hope that I might get laid, got me out of bed and to my own door. I opened it a crack and saw a woman trying to get herself organized.

"Do you need help?" I asked.

She turned towards me.

Jesus Christ, it's Lard-Ass.

Sure enough, she had fallen the next rung down the ladder of survival.

"What?" she asked, her voice angry but her eyes almost smiling.

"Help, do you need any?"

"Could I use your john?"

Now that's a great double entendre.

"Sure." I opened the door.

"Do I know you?" she peered into my face. "I've seen you before."

I played dumb. I hoped she wouldn't remember the alley and my pathetic attempt to talk with her. "I doubt it. I've never been to Baltimore before."

"How about New York?"

"Yeah, sure. I live there."

"Ever go for some exotic dancing?"

"On occasion."

"The Golden Swan?"

"I can't remember the names. Possibly."

I did remember, and that wasn't the place, not by a long shot. The Golden Swan was a class act with a cover and high-priced, watered-down drinks. If she ever worked there, it was long before I'd seen her.

"Did you work there?"

"Yeah." She breezed it out as if defying me to contradict her.

A little stroking was in order. "Probably too rich for my pocketbook."

Taking in the frayed condition of my underwear, she said, "Yeah, I can see that."

I pointed to the bathroom door. "Help yourself."

"Thanks," she waltzed across the room like she was Marlene Dietrich.

I wanted to laugh at her pretension, but I wanted to get laid even more. "You got a name?" I asked as she reached the bathroom door.

"Sue."

"Nick."

"So hello, Nick."

"So hello, Sue. You into spending the night?"

"For sixty bucks."

Fuck me, more than the guy next door.

No haggling. Not wanting to let on that I had listened. She wanted sixty bucks, I'd give her sixty bucks. I felt a twinge of guilt using Mo's money for a hooker, but I really needed something to make me feel better. And she had to be better than that crummy sandwich.

For all of her droopiness, Sue was still in good feminine condition. She knew how to use her hands and voice to cajole and flatter until I felt like she really loved me and wanted it. She didn't stay the night, but I was well satisfied by the time we finished. I had paid her the sixty upfront. As she was leaving, I pulled my wallet from the nightstand and took out another ten.

"What's this for?" she asked.

"For making me feel good."

"Thanks," Sue made a point of tucking it into her ample cleavage so I could have one parting thrill. She smiled at me. Her eyes, her light lime-green eyes, twinkled.

As she closed the door, I remembered those eyes and I remembered Estrella.

The same.

The same lime eyes.

I lay on the bed and smoked one more cigarette, then fell into the pitching, tossing sleep of the hapless.

Chapter 20: Back Home

The bright sun reflected blinding white off the snow that had not yet turned to the grime and gray of Charm City—the last thing I would have called Baltimore. The dazzling light of that next morning belied the fears and doubts which still lingered in my mind. I found Quick-Pics, a sixty-minute photo shop, and had my film developed. "Two sets for the price of one," the sign read.

Good deal, one for Mo and one for me.

While they worked on my photographs, I got myself a mediocre non-New York bagel and a decent cup of coffee and read *The New York Times*.

The Have-A-Cup was busy, customers taking quick breaks from the biting, sparkling cold, and waitresses refilling cups, taking orders, rushing plates of eggs, toast, potatoes to impatient patrons.

"Where's my bacon?"

"I asked for an English muffin."

I might as well have been on a secluded island. I willed myself far from the drama and danger that had filled the day before. I felt anonymous and unnoticed except by the waitress. Having written down my order, she demanded I pay in advance, a cruel testimony to my bedraggled appearance.

With some modicum of sanity restored, I picked up the pictures and headed for the train station.

The shoving stream of people trying to travel through a major snowstorm had dwindled to almost nothing. The station was quiet. There would be a train to New York in less than half an hour, which gave me time for another cup of coffee and a cigarette.

I looked through the photos and understood nothing. I wondered if Mo would get anything more.

The train was almost empty, a much appreciated change from the steamy, overflowing mob scene of the day before. As we pulled out of the city and headed for Wilmington, I looked out the dirty window and admired the white tree branches and the incredibly blue sky. Nature had transformed herself from menace to pacific beauty. I unfolded my *Times* and resumed reading.

Truth: behind that printed screen I am replaying the night. My palms feel the cupping of Sue's breasts. My tongue still tastes her flavor. My nipple still stings from her bite.

Lost in myself I was aware of neither jolts nor lurches as the miles clacked away under those wheels of steel. Through Philadelphia, up the length of New Jersey, under the Hudson River, the train roared while I daydreamed, occasionally smoked, and constantly thought about the lard-assed whore with whom I had made love the night before. I thought about her eyes and about Estrella's.

I thought about what I had done that far-away evening in Chile and hoped Estrella had forgiven me. I hoped she had gotten over it. I hoped she thought of me all the damn time.

I called Mo from Penn Station. "Did you get the photos developed?" he asked.

"Yeah, in Baltimore."

"I want to see them. Bring both sets."

How the hell did he ...

Mo wanted to meet right away. I put him off 'til lunch the next day. I realized there was something I had to do first.

"Just be sure to bring all your pictures," he instructed.

"Some are—"

"Bring them all, both sets."

"You already said—"

"And, Nick."

"Yeah?"

"Bring the film."

I called Emily to tell her that I was still sick and wouldn't be in for another day. She pissed and moaned a bit, but a guy has the right to get sick once in a while. I certainly wasn't going to tell her the truth, that I had been chasing my Pulitzer in the snowy suburbs of Washington, D.C.

"Are you home?" she asked, obviously trying to trip me up.

"No. I'm still at my aunt's." My excuse before I had left for Washington.

"Why don't you give me the number?"

"One of her rules," I lied. "Sorry, but no can do. Hopefully I can get in tomorrow."

"You'd better. The work is piling up."

"I know," I coughed for effect. "I have to go." Coughed again. "Bathroom. Really got to go."

I hung up sure I had played the part well.

I figured Emily would try star sixty-nine only to learn that the calling phone couldn't be reached that way.

Auntie has a blocked line. Got to remember that in case she asks.

I didn't mind having to rush to catch up once I got back to work. I did mind losing two days' pay, which was a hell of a lot more than I could afford to give up.

Instead of the subway, I decided to leave the catacombs and walk part of the way to Brooklyn. The mad rush of the city was underway. As they always do, New Yorkers had dug themselves out and gotten right back to work.

The beauty of winter was already gone. Gray slush and dirty water were everywhere. Taxis and trucks splashed along, happily oblivious to the soggy pedestrians who cursed after them.

When I got back to the apartment, I took a long, hot shower, shaved slowly and carefully, and changed into clean clothes. I stole a glass of one of my roommate's milk and some cookies, dragged a brown, overstuffed armchair, which had come with the rent control, to the window and sat staring at nothing, my mind unfocused, my weary eyes emptily watching winter.

I was hoping to drift back, to recapture one of those wonderful snow days from my youth. But, all I could do was to dwell on Sue, relive and relive again our sexual encounter, see and see again her eyes, her lime eyes, her Estrella eyes, eyes that twinkled in the black night of my soul.

I always enjoyed the reminiscence of sex more than the act itself. In my daydreams Sue became more attractive and a better, more eager lover. I became the super stud every man longs to be. I knew that I was fooling myself, but hey, who did it hurt?

Fantasy is a friendly refuge for the inadequate.

The phone rang. Instead of picking up, I turned up the answering machine. My gay roommate's mother bitched he hadn't written or called.

Don't complain, lady. Do you really want to know what he's doing? Where his cock has been?

Another call. This one my editor. Emily was not the trusting type. She said she was calling to see how I was doing. In reality, she was seeing if she could catch me in my lie.

I wasn't angry that she didn't trust me. Hell, she was right. I was just pissed that she had interrupted my daydreams—fantasy interruptus.

"Fooled you, bitch," I said to the dust. "I told you I was at my aunt's." The thought of that little victory kept me company for the rest of the afternoon.

Hopefully she's on her way home. I don't want her around when I get to the office.

Three in the morning I subwayed to the paper. There was something that had to be done before my lunch meeting with Mo.

It took fifteen minutes for the copier to warm up. I used the time to see if there was anything interesting in the pile of notes on my desk. Most were from Emily, do-this-get-to-that-notes.

"Somebody named Melinda called. Wanted to know if you were alive. Told her I didn't know, that you'd been out. New girlfriend?"

Fuck. Maybe there's still a—Fuck it.

I pulled the photos from the Quick-Pic envelope. The machine hummed as I made my duplicates.

No way Mo will know about this set. No way Mo is getting them all.

Chapter 21: Enemies Connected

As we'd agreed, Mo was waiting at my favorite hamburger joint. After Washington, I felt entitled to a reward.

I'm not going to tell Mo about Sue. If he asks for receipts, I'll make up a story.

I hoped Mo would treat me to a bacon cheeseburger, which he'd then have to watch me eat. On the subway I imagined the bacon grease dripping down my chin and his reactions.

As soon as I sat down, he held out his hand for the photos.

I handed him one set of pictures and the negatives.

"The other set," He held out his hand again.

Got you. I knew that was coming.

Without a word, I complied.

Silently, Mo studied the photographs. I looked around for the waiter.

"I already ordered."

"Huh?"

"Don't worry, I ordered your favorite."

"My favorite?"

"Yeah, bacon cheese with everything, double bacon, crispy fries, and a Coke. Right?"

I nodded.

We had never been there together.

Has be been following me?

I stared hard at him.

Mo looked up from the photographs, saw my expression, and, as if he could read my mind, matter-of-factly commented, "I've been covering your ass for a while."

"What? Why?"

"You've gotten into some pretty heavy water, and it's likely to get stormier." He turned back to the photos.

The waiter brought me a bacon-cheese with extra bacon, well-done fries, a Coke and a coffee. I dumped sugar packets into the coffee and stirred.

Shit, he doesn't miss a trick.

"I hope you don't mind."

"What?"

"I ordered the bacon well-done."

Son of a bitch, no greasy chin.

"Yeah, that will be fine."

Mo had ordered tea for himself. He looked at the Lipton bag with disdain before dunking it into the steaming water. "Americans," he muttered.

I said nothing.

"Where were these taken?" Mo shoved the two pictures of the clown in the green suit across the table.

"On the train. He was sitting next to me and I had leftover—"

"And this guy?"

"What he looks like, the conductor. Last shot on the roll." He put the three pictures back into the pile of photographs and went through it again.

I had half eaten my burger before Mo looked up again. He took a sip of tea and said, "This is worse than I thought."

I nearly choked. I had never before heard that tone in his voice—at once cold and anxious.

He shuffled the pictures and went back to studying them. Took two out of the mix, looked at one, looked at the next, and went back to the first.

What the hell is happening? Holy fuck, will we both be dead in an hour?

Cold needles pushed into my spine. I could feel a weight on my shoulders.

Mo must have seen me squirming. He changed topics. "Must have been a rough trip?"

My guts churned. I tried to be nonchalant. "The snow kind of sucked."

"Maybe it helped. They may have been less vigilant. Otherwise—"

"Who are they?"

"Government people."

"CIA?"

"What makes you ...? Yeah, CIA, NSA, and maybe some others. Your country has made its government into alphabet soup."

"Not all of them?"

"What?"

"Government. They're not all government?"

"No, there were others."

"The Mob?" I asked, knowing and dreading the answer.

"They're involved."

"Burmaste."

"The mayor's boy?" Mo looked up suddenly.

"Yeah, I saw him. He was there. In the pictures. Is he CIA?"

"Not exactly, but he's connected to them. Since Cuba I would guess. And of course he's also—"

"Mobbed up?"

"Yeah."

"One happy family." I took a giant bite of burger, chewed for a minute, and then, burger juices dripping from the corner of my mouth, asked, "Was he a spy in Cuba?"

"No, not likely. The CIA really got involved after Castro. Then came the Bay of Pigs. Ever hear of it?"

I was embarrassed to admit I hadn't. I'd enjoyed American History in high school but had never taken a college class. The high school textbook stopped at Korea. No Vietnam, no Bay of Pigs, no Kennedy assassination, no Granada, Panama, the list goes on, school funding does not. Mo filled me in on the story, Kennedy staring down Khrushchev or maybe just reaching an agreement.

"Did Cuba have him assassinated?" I asked when he took a break to fiddle with his cup.

"Who knows? I just know it wasn't Israel." He barked a quick laugh.

I saw nothing to laugh at. "So where does Burmaste fit in? How did he get connected to the CIA?"

"Around the Bay of Pigs. A lot of ex-patriot Cubans ended up working for the agency. With time, paranoia about Castro took over D.C. By the time Burmaste came to the States, Washington would hire any Cuban who had a halfway convincing story. Your government had persuaded itself that Castro and his little island were going to bring you all to your knees—that he was going to launch some kind of terror campaign, or missiles, or maybe a revolution."

"But Burmaste works for the mayor now?" I interrupted. While I could easily accept Burmaste's mob connections, it seemed impossible that a player in New York City politics was also involved with the CIA.

"So he does, but a man can have two masters, maybe even more." He picked up the tea, which had long since gone cold, and looked deeply into the cup. He put it down with a disgusted glare.

"I don't get any of this."

"Someday, maybe you will. For now, it's probably just as well that you don't."

"I ..."

I started again. "There was one guy. He looked like an Arab or some kind of Middle Easterner."

"Yeah. I saw. An Arab, you were right on that."

"Do you know who he is?" I could feel my voice beginning to shake. I stuffed fries into my face hoping the act of chewing would calm me.

Ketchup dripped down my chin.

Mo pulled a napkin from the holder and held it towards me. "Wipe your chin."

So much for the bacon.

"Thanks," I took the napkin and did as he instructed.

The burger had gone cold. The next bite felt like it was congealing into a lump in my throat.

"Do you know who he is?" I repeated. "The Arab," I added.

"Yeah." There was grimness in Mo's voice.

"Who?"

"They think he loves them, but he only loves their money and playing them. That's the big thing, playing them."

"Who?"

"You're better off not knowing." Mo's tone made it clear that there could be no discussion.

"I don't get it. Mo, I can't understand any of this."

"Like I said, you're better off." Mo slipped the photos into his pocket. "And, you're better off not having these."

"Damn, how do I write a story if I don't know—"

Mo started whistling. It was the same tune he had whistled in Peru.

I spoke over the sound. "This guy, is he part of your job? Part of the reason you're here in the States?"

With a quick nod, Mo handed me a wad of cash. I had hoped that he would let me keep the meager change from my adventure, but the small roll of twenties he was trying to give me was embarrassing. "I—"

"It's your pay." He pushed the cash deeper into my hand.

"Pay?"

"Consider yourself an agent." He winked, the same wink he had used that frightening night in Peru.

Mo got up and moved away from the booth. Turning back to me, he smiled. "Don't forget to pay for my tea."

"I've got it covered," I answered, feeling as stupid as I knew how.

Chapter 22: Delaying the Inevitable

I had never thought much about death. In high school a few kids I knew, not close friends, just kids I knew, had overdosed. One committed suicide, jumped in front of a train, but my friends and I were too stoned to deal with that shit. We just sat around with a dube and talked about how cool it all was that they were dead and no longer had the hassles of school and parents.

Three of my grandparents died by the time I was two. I have no memory of them. The last grandparent, my paternal grandmother, the one of the parking lot lineage, hung around until I was fourteen, zany and conservative at the same time. As a kid, I thought she was pretty neat. It never occurred to me she'd die, just seemed she'd live forever. She passed. I was too busy playing cool to react.

When I got home from meeting Mo, I was weirded-out. I imagined all kinds of things: that he was having me followed, that Burmaste and company were going to kill me, that the mob was in wait around every corner. The list went on and on. The idea of my own mortality was more than I could handle. I wanted to get high. It had been a long time, and I knew it wasn't an answer. I still wanted it.

I also wanted to run away, but I had nowhere to go. Big as it was, Mo's wad of twenties wouldn't get me there anyway.

I fidgeted and obsessed. My thoughts kept returning to John Hunter, the man who didn't exist but who had bought an old school in the Lower East Side of New York. The guy was somehow connected to everything, and that everything seemed evil, threatening, and murderous. I wanted to go to Hunter's place and demand an explanation. As if the spook making believe he was Hunter could explain anything. As if the address on all those papers really was his home or even his office.

Most of all, I wanted to get laid.

When scared enough, sex beats Valium.

I would gladly have paid Sue with her big ass and green eyes another sixty, but how to reach her?

Did she come back to New York or is she still in Baltimore? Hell, what was she doing in Baltimore anyway?

Absent Sue, I wanted to call Melinda. Maybe we could get it together for just one night. I fought off the impulse, but it kept coming back. I dialed. Her phone rang once. I hung up.

I hadn't seen Melinda for a while. Partly, I had avoided her. Partly, our paths were crossing less and less. She hadn't been at the community center much. Jose and David, faced with the unpleasant reality, were telling the various programs to wind down, and that meant less for volunteers like Melinda to do.

The interminable court battles were still going on. The mythical John Hunter had not yet taken physical possession. But the handwriting was on the wall. Jose's delaying tactics could only last so long.

Jose had to have the Community Center running in order to maintain the necessary legal standing to keep up the court challenges. Without standing it would be impossible for him to seek the court orders that would at least delay the construction projects that were dotting Alphabet City, all those construction projects that were eventually going to come crashing down.

Jose hoped that the delays would last long enough for the new buildings, the ones he had been unable to delay, to start sinking and collapsing. The first set of condominiums was half occupied and all sold. But that wasn't a high-rise. It was a beautiful piece of development, the perfect bait for the eventual bait-and-switch. The more expensive high-rise condos, which were not yet finished, were already being marketed, as were the rentals, which would include the legally requisite number of low-income units. Investors were clamoring to buy those rental buildings, and merchants were equally excited about the retail spaces that were to come. Everybody was chasing pie in the sky, the great American dream.

It was Jose's hope that this Alphabet City pie, constructed as it was of greed and deception, would collapse in the oven. If only he could hold out long enough. He was nothing if not tenacious. It was possible, barely possible, he might just win. People in the know pointed out the cracks that were appearing in brand-new structures, even as they rose from the ground. Surreptitiously, Jose and his friends photographed and measured those cracks, making a notation and probably chortling each time one expanded.

They also measured the settling that was ever so slowly starting. Concrete piles had been placed beneath the new buildings. But those piles had no real footing; they simply ended somewhere in the sifting sand the East River had deposited over the centuries. Even the low-rise buildings were settling. It was only fractions of centimeters so far, but Jose was sure that with time the sinking would accelerate.

"Delay, delay, delay," he described his strategy. "Delay and let nature take its course. I gotta tell ya, the only question is will our time run out before it happens."

Delaying. That was what I was doing, too. I was delaying the inevitable second call to Melinda. I was embarrassed, but I needed some kind of confirmation that I existed, that I was alive, that I was there. I knew Mo would be angry. Did I care? I knew that Melinda might refuse me. I didn't care about that either. I needed sex, wonderful, anxiety-reducing sex.

Much better than Xanex.

Nature is inevitable. Inevitably those buildings would sink into the sand waiting beneath them. Death, also, is inevitable. My death was inevitable. That was certain, and for the first time in my life I realized it. The thought terrified me. Terror is inevitable, too. It comes with being human. From deep within me there bubbled a response to that terror. I suppose it was as inevitable as all the rest. I picked up the phone again.

Chapter 23: Nightmares

The island of Manhattan is in many ways a wonder of nature and of man. Most of it foots on granite. Rising up from that fortress of stone are the skyscrapers through which much of the world's business flows.

The people of Manhattan are also a wonder of nature. Rushing about, trying desperately to not notice each other, yet always, subconsciously, measuring themselves one against the next. Their capacity to selectively ignore the pulsing stimulation around them defies logic.

If the world were an animal, Manhattan would have to be its heart. But, what a cold heart it would be.

That night, traveling to Melinda's, aware that I was going to have sex with my friend's girl, I felt organically a part of the city. It was such a New York thing to do.

What a stupid rationalization. Did I believe it? Who knows? At that moment, more than anything else, I needed the clasp of a woman's legs around my thighs, her pussy around me, her arms around my neck. Any woman would have done as long as I could feel safe with her. Melinda was the woman who was available.

I thought about Sue and wished she were there. Even Marcie would have done the job, at least I wouldn't be going behind Mo's back. And I wouldn't have to cope with the freezing, cold wind off the river, cold that was turning the streets to ice, or with the dankness of the subway that cut through my bones. I wouldn't have to deal with the fetid scurrying of the subway's resident rats, that inevitable symbol of all the evil that lies hidden beneath. Hiding in wait for what? Perhaps for us all.

I realized Marcie had been a good thing for me. She may have become boring, still, she had been comfortable, safe, and always available. But she became a thing—not a person, not an equal—a thing of comfort like a child's blanket.

My uncle Ham, actually my mother's uncle, a wry buzzard of a man who hung on interminably in a nursing home in The Bronx, always talked about the joys of travel, the zest of adventure. He had encouraged me to go to Chile and urged me to see much of South America. That's when I told him about Deidre, the hot Dominica with her hungry crabs. That was the kind of thing I could tell Uncle Ham, stuff I could never tell Dad.

"She may be a fruitcake, Nicolas, but at least your mother lives. She isn't afraid to jump. Life is a risk, boy."

For all his talk, Uncle Ham had done very little traveling. An unadventurous adventurer, he collected globes and maps, read books about the most inaccessible countries with the excitement of a first-time tourist, but he went nowhere.

Braving that winter night to relieve my panic by the animal act of sex, I wished I could be more like my great-uncle. I wished I could content myself by curling up in front of a television with a good piece of pornography and a cup of cocoa. I wished I could sublimate the need to chase a Pulitzer, the need that had led me into the midst of terror, sublimate it into pursuing some eccentric collection. I wished, too, I had decided to follow my father and his father into the parking business, into something safe in which I would only have to deal with the mob. I wished I had never met Jose, that I had never lived in Alphabet City, that I was not off to cheat on my buddy, and that the Pulitzer story I was chasing was nothing but a dream. In my fear and discomfort I wished and wished.

Wishing never makes things so.

The train plunged through the rat-infested tunnels of the night, and I cursed myself for being on it at the same time that my brainless member cursed it for being too slow.

Melinda opened the door. I threw myself at her. The force of my entry carried us across the room and onto the soft comfort of her beige couch. I wanted to rip off her clothes and mine. Instead, I contented myself with a deep kiss, forcing my tongue into her mouth where it met the silky softness of hers. My arms wove around her like tentacles. My hands were touching, groping, pulling as if they had a life of their own.

Melinda didn't resist, only whispered that I should take off my coat, that it was icy cold against her body. I stood, shucked off the offending coat, my muffler, and hat with a series of jerky motions. The impulse, the need, the desire was too great to contain.

We had sex on the couch and again rolling onto the floor. The adrenalin reservoir built over the past two days exploded in multiple orgasms. At some point, I cannot remember exactly when, Melinda invited me to spend the night. We lay in her queen-sized bed with its silk sheets and soft, down pillows and held hands. No more sex, no more acrobatics of desire, just a simple act of togetherness.

The relief of stupor spread over me. Sleep descended in that wonderful half-conscious way it sometimes does. My eyelids grew heavy. I no longer had the will to see. My arms and legs slowly turned to numbness. There was no purpose in moving them. Then came rest, gentle, sweet repose.

My sleep, so soothingly entered, ended with a nightmare.

I dreamed of Easter Island.

My father and I had flown there from Santiago. It had been one of his childhood fantasies to see the giant statues, those great unexplained monuments of a long since disappeared culture. We hiked, stared, and took pictures. We asked other tourists to take pictures of us. Like all tourists to the island, we wondered how the giant statues had been moved and why they had been created.

We stayed in a quiet pensione and enjoyed being together. It had been one of those times I truly loved the old man, not just his money. We bonded, father and son. It had been a positive time, a time of possibilities waiting like great mysteries to be discovered.

In my nightmare the great *figuras* surrounded me. They had come alive and carried giant, if ancient, weapons: spears, axes, maces, swords, pikes. Slowly but relentlessly, they advanced towards me. I stood, unarmed and nude, an erection and nothing else to protect me. One of the statues banged an immense gong. My body shook in time with its reverberations.

Melinda's phone rang. It was three o'clock.

What a shitty time for a phone call.

Still in the haze of sleep, Melinda picked up the receiver. "Hello."

She listened for a moment. "Oh, my God! No! Oh, my God."

She listened again. "Do they know who?"

A pause.

"Of course."

Another pause.

"No, that's all right."

"Yes, I'll let him know."

"I'll make some calls."

"Is anybody with her?"

"Do you want me to meet you there?"

"Tell her ... God, I don't know what to say."

"Yes, of course. Tomorrow." She put the receiver down. There were tears streaming down her face.

"What is it?" I asked.

"Jose," she managed.

"What about him?"

"He's dead."

I felt like I'd been hit by one of those wrecking balls working their way through Alphabet City. "What?"

"He's dead. Jose. Somebody murdered him."

"Murdered?" I couldn't think of anything else to say. There was a long pause before she continued.

"Bashed his head in with a rock."

"Who? Where?"

"It's Saturday night; he was at Maria's. He went out for his smoke. Some ... somebody murdered him. Some bastard murdered him. They murdered a saint, a god-damn saint."

"Who?" It was all I could think to say.

"Helen."

"Helen murdered him?"

That makes no sense.

"No. I don't know who. Helen didn't know."

"That was Helen on the phone?"

"Of course."

"Of course," I echoed as if I was saying something intelligent.

Chapter 24: Hurt

Melinda cried big, gulping, distraught tears. I wrapped my arms around her. "It'll be okay. It'll be okay," I crooned over and over. I knew better, but I said it anyway and wished it were true.

Wishing never makes things so.

After a time, Melinda, nestled against my breast, quieted. I held her tightly.

Nothing like comforting a crying woman to make a man feel big.

And she held me.

We breathed as one. Our hearts beat as one. Joined by shock and sorrow, we lay there in the strange harmony of pain.

The silence held the softness of clouds. Had someone walked in on us, we would have looked misleadingly peaceful. We lay there in a strange pain-filled silence.

We held one another for hours.

We never spoke of that night again. I don't know what Melinda was thinking.

I thought about Jose Figurés. I replayed the evening I had spent with him and Maria. I saw the photographs on Maria's walls. I tasted the meal she'd made. In my mind I again took the short walk Jose and I had taken after supper, Jose's regular, clockwork smoke walk.

I pictured Jose lying on the ground, blood flowing from his head, melting the dirty snow that was still covering the grass around town, the blood congealing into its own red ice.

I was not sure what Jose and my relationship had been. We were friendly, but not friends. The difference in our ages was great. Our backgrounds were totally dissimilar. Our goals in life completely different.

Neither were we colleagues. The Community Center had been his life. Through it he had hoped to save the world, or at least his corner of it. Me? I wanted to become famous, a Pulitzer Prize winner. Someday I wanted to read my obituary in *The Times*. If I did good for the world in the process, that would be okay. But the fame, the prize, the glory was everything.

Then it hit me: Jose was my challenge, more than a challenge, an opportunity. I had hoped to expose the moneymaking schemers who were so ready to tear down Alphabet City and build doomed projects. I had thought that was going to be a good story, good enough to move me up the ranks of reporters and get me a job at one of the real papers, and Jose represented that challenge. Not the way Sacks, my high school principal, had been a challenge, to show him up, but still a challenge.

I heard Jose's voice. It had been the day we met John Hunter, whoever he was.

"You're a damn reporter aren't you? Then you be in the way. That's your job."

Now Jose was dead—murdered. I had no doubts that his death was tied to his opposition to the construction companies and their mob-related money. If I could break the story I would be on my way, maybe even with a couple Pulitzers in hand.

I don't know if Melinda or I ever fell back into real sleep. When I realized it was morning, my arms were still wrapped around her. We hadn't moved. A part of me didn't want to move, not then, not ever. Another part screamed to get up, to investigate, to report, to become a great journalist.

Thinking Melinda was still asleep, I buried my face in the nape of her neck and tried to force myself to doze off. She stirred at the touch and asked if I was awake.

Grudgingly, I answered.

While I showered, Melinda made coffee and toasted a couple of frozen bagels. We ate in silence, our thoughts caught in the phone call that was certainly going to change our lives.

"We ought to get to the Center," she said.

"Or to Queens."

"No, I think Maria has enough on her plate right now. She doesn't need people trying to help. We'd only make things worse."

"Not to her place. I was thinking of the police. See if we can find out what's going on."

"Are you a reporter or a friend?"

"Both."

I wanted to get to Frank O'Marra and learn the police scuttlebutt before any curtain of secrecy might fall. As much as I hated to admit it, I also had to get to the office or Emily would have my ass. I had already missed too many of those stupid assignments and taken too many sick days. Maybe Frank could help me redeem myself with a couple juicy tidbits.

"Do what you want." Melinda's voice had grown cold. "Last night was a mistake anyway."

"What the hell does that mean?"

"It means what it means."

"I hate it when women talk in riddles."

"Personally, I think you just hate women."

"Because I don't want to go to the Center?"

"Because …." She paused and changed direction. "Look, it was a mistake. We've been there before. It didn't work. Remember?"

"I remember, but I also remember that what we had was great when it did work. That last night was great, at least until—"

"It was fine." The word fine, delivered in a staccato burst, crushed me. "But you're not the right guy for me."

"And, I suppose Mo is?"

"Mo? What are you talking about? We broke up a week ago. I would never … you thought I'd … while I was actually going with someone? I'm not some whore."

"I know that."

"The hell you do. You think every woman is a whore … a skank, a bitch and a prostitute. God, you hate women and you don't even know it." She pushed me out of her apartment with, "Fuck you."

"I'm sorry," I said to the closing door.

I heard her response through the wood. "That's for damn sure."

Her words stung.

Why does the truth always have barbs?

I headed towards the subway and Queens.

Chapter 25: Bullshit

"Drug pushers?"

It was late afternoon before I could get together with Frank O'Marra. Reluctantly, he acknowledged my presence.

Still pissed about Hunter. If he only knew. Better he not; he would never talk to me again.

"Can I buy you one?" I gestured towards his beer.

Frank shrugged. I signaled Mahatma, who brought two bottles.

So, buddy, what do you know about this Figurés murder?"

"I ain't your buddy."

I knew to not respond.

He nursed his brew, maybe hoping I'd disappear, maybe not caring. Finally, his two word answer, "Drug pushers."

"That makes no sense. Figurés wasn't involved with drugs."

"No, but he was involved with fighting them."

"Not in this neighborhood. He came up there to relax, not to do social work."

"Sounds like you was friends?"

"We were. Well sort of. Good acquaintances." I wasn't going to lie and risk losing my police contact, minimal as it was, but I wasn't going to tell him any more than necessary. "I even went to his wife's place for supper one weekend. I know he came up here to chill."

"Well, that ain't what we hear on the street. He was passing out leaflets and that some of the pushers got bent."

Over some anti-drug leaflets?

I drew out my response. "I won-n-n-der. Look, if you hear anything, will you let me know? My bitch of an editor is ready to can my ass. I need a real story."

"Yeah, sure, long as you're buying. But I don't think you're going to get much. Around here a bunch of druggies doing something senseless ain't exactly what you newspaper guys would call *fresh*."

"Maybe not, but I want to know. Call it a personal thing. He was a nice guy."

If I tell him about the Washington connection, Frank will run like a rabbit.

"Sure, if you say so."

I paid for his beer and mine and got up to leave.

"Hey, you didn't finish your beer."

Maybe Frank was feeling sociable, but not me. I turned back and took another swig. Setting the bottle back on the bar, I said, "I got work to catch up on, and I want to get over to see Maria."

"Maria?"

"Jose's wife."

"I didn't even know his first name, and you know hers. But, I have some advice. If I were you, I don't know if I'd go over there tonight."

"How come?"

"I'm sure the detectives will be interviewing her."

"I thought they had it all figured out."

"I didn't say that. That's their theory right now."

"The theory of the crime?" I tried to keep my sarcasm out of my voice.

"Exactly. But, they still have to do a full investigation."

"Well, I think I should stop by anyway just to let her know … give her moral support, that kind of thing."

"Suit yourself."

Does he know something? Why would detectives be … what the hell is going on?

Not convinced I had fully mined my source, I squatted on a stool and picked up my half-emptied bottle. "It really sucks."

"What?"

"That good guys get killed by junk-pushing bastards."

"That's for sure."

"Assuming it was pushers. Could it have been a simple robbery?" I asked.

"Except that his wallet weren't taken."

"So whoever killed him did it because they wanted him dead."

"Yeah, Nick, that's a reasonable conclusion."

"Frank, that seems a bit over the top?"

"What do you mean? Somebody kills you they want you dead."

"Sure, but … well, that Jose was just passing around leaflets and they bopped him? Does that make sense?"

"Like I said, druggies never do."

Chapter 26: Women in Mourning

I didn't drop by to see Maria that night. The pile of work held me captive in the office, and the thought of detectives swarming through her apartment put me off. Instead, I called her from Brooklyn the next day, expressed my condolences, and asked what she might know.

She poured out a tale of woe and anger. "They grilled me like I was a suspect. My husband is murdered, and they don't have no respect. *Es un buen hombre.*"

"I know. He was a great guy."

"All the police wanted was to look at his papers and shit, like he was hiding something. Why would he? My Jose never did anything wrong. *No tenía nada que ocultar*, nothing, Nick, I swear it. What did they want from me?"

"It sounds awful, Maria. I know they have to do their job, but damn. Just awful."

"It was. They wanted to search the apartment. I told them go ahead. They messed it up. Didn't put nothing back. Didn't offer to help. I couldn't sleep till it was back in order. I was up until three thirty. Know what they found?"

"No, what?"

"A few leftover papers they said were from last week."

"What kind of papers?"

"The kind you put up on telephone poles."

"Flyers?"

"Yeah. Right. Flyers. About drugs and how people should be reporting pushers to the cops. The cops said that Jose hung them around last week for the community board. Like somebody killed him for that. I don't even remember him doing it. How many could he have put up? We got better things to do weekends."

"I know." I tried to not be indecent with my imaginings of her and Jose. "But there were flyers up?"

"Of course, there are always flyers. Every weekend. There are always people putting up flyers. Flyers for everything. Lots of them about drugs. *Todo para bien.* Like a piece of paper is gonna stop the drugs. But, they keep trying. Just like they keep trying to get people to stop dumping their shit on the streets.

"What I don't understand is how dumb can the police get? The druggies are gonna kill one guy, my Jose. Why? I ask you, why? Even if he did put some of those papers up, why would they kill him?"

"I have no idea." I paused for a moment in case she wanted to say more. She didn't.

"Did they mention any specific suspects?"

"No one. They asked if I knew anyone. Any enemies."

"What did you say?"

"The truth. I told them the mayor, Burmaste, the contractors down in Alphabet City. Hell, for all the damn good it did, I named them all. The cops just laughed. 'Sure the Mayor put a hit out on him. Why not the Pope?' That's what one cop said. I told him the Pope didn't have no money invested in those damn buildings downtown.

"He laughed. My husband's dead, and this cop is laughing like I told him a joke. *Mi marido está muerto y todo lo que él puede hacer es reírse.*"

"I guess the cops want it to be easy, a nice, simple, local crime."

"They said they was going down to the Center to look around, but what I think? They'll get some local scumbag they can pick up easy and frame easy. That's the cops for you. *¿Por qué trabajar cuando no have falta?*"

"You may well be right. We have to wait and see what they do."

"Do. They'll do what they always do, as little as possible. A Latino gets killed, they don't care. "

There was silence. I tried to visualize Maria, tears in her eyes but anger and steel in her soul.

"*¿Un buen hombre ha muerto, le importa?*" she asked.

The police care? No. I'd guess not.

"Maria, is there anything I can do for you?"

"Make them find my husband's killer."

"Make them? Who?"

"The cops. Make them."

"How?"

"You're a reporter, aren't you?"

"Sure, on a tiny, local paper."

"I don't care. You're a reporter. Keep after them until they find the *bastardos*." The passion in Maria's voice singed the telephone wires. The tears in her words drowned my heart. I felt overwhelmed by the responsibility Maria was laying on me even though it had been my plan all along.

"I—"

"Do your best. Make Jose proud of you. He deserves that. Make him proud."

"I will. I promise."

"*¡Que Dios le bendiga!*"

Her tears broke through and filled the connection between us. I could feel my own eyes welling up. Unable to say more and with nothing more to say I managed, "*Adios*."

My next call was to Helen. The police hadn't been at the Center yet. *What is taking them so long? Oh, yeah, why work when you can do it easy?*

"I don't think they consider it necessary. They've got this theory about some local guys. If the cops run true-to-form, they're going to make that stick," Helen said.

"'Make it stick.' What does that mean?"

"It means they'll find a way to get the evidence they want. They'll find some patsies and prove them guilty."

"Even if they're innocent?"

"Since when does that mater to cops? You haven't been around the Hispanic community much. Look what they did to The Latins."

"I know. But—"

"But nothing. The cops figure a Latino's life isn't worth shit."

"Jose is … was a public figure."

"He was still an Hispanic, a P.R., which is to say not worth shit. They'll sweep it under the carpet and fuck us and this community." Along with tears there was rage in Helen's voice. She and Maria had both lost the core of their lives.

"You and Maria think alike, that the cops will just go through the motions."

"Of course we do. We've been with Jose for years. How many times have we seen how it works?"

"Look, let me know when they show up down there, that is, if they show up."

"Oh, they'll show. They'll show up to put us out on the street. Hunter will show up to with a whole pack of those lying bastards."

"Yeah, he might. Just try to keep your cool. Don't get yourself arrested."

"My mother didn't raise an idiot. Just take care of yourself."

"They don't arrest reporters."

"Yeah, sure." She coughed a bit uncomfortably. "But, they do kill them."

The return of an unwelcome thought.

I sat in the ugly brown chair next to the phone and stared at the faded pattern of the rug for what seemed like hours.

John Hunter.

John Hunter.

I could visualize him: tall, thin, owlish glasses, expensive clothes.

But he's not really John Hunter. John Hunter's a myth, and John Hunter, the guy who does not exist, the guy who will dispossess Jose Figurés, one of the best men I ever met. Now Jose is dead and the cops are going to help Hunter. There is something really fucked up here.

Chapter 27: Lawyering Up

The police did visit the center, eventually, two days after Jose's funeral. Two days after the overflowing mass at St. Margaret's, the unassuming church where Maria and Jose had been married. Maria insisted the funeral mass be said there, in Queens, far from Alphabet City.

Distance didn't stop the people whose lives Jose had worked so hard to improve, whose community he had tried so hard to save. They flowed off the subway and onto the unfamiliar streets of Queens. They came in their best clothes, bearing flowers and tears. Quietly, they filled the pews: hard-worked men and women, people whose tattoos proclaimed that they had served time, elderly people, children. They filled the church and they lined the street as the hearse pulled away.

The hearse was escorted by Latins in full gang regalia on roaring bikes. Julio Martinez was a pallbearer, his wife, Angelina, sat behind Maria with her hand on the widow's shoulder. Helen was on one side of Maria and Maria's son, Miguel, was on the other. Maria's daughter was represented by an outsized wreath of bright flowers.

I took pictures and asked people about Jose. Emily, impressed by the turnout, allowed me to write an article about the funeral, not about the crime or the Community Center, but about the turnout and about the man who was so beloved.

"Make it something the community can be proud of," she instructed, ignoring the reality that hundreds of the mourners had come from another part of the city. The editor of our little weekly didn't want to know anything about Alphabet City. She certainly wasn't going to consider the connection between Jose's death and the controversy in which he was a central figure.

"Local news is just that," she said, "local. Keep it focused at home."

If she were the editor of the Springfield, Illinois *Gazette*, Lincoln's death would have been reported, "Local Man Killed in Washington", I commented to Pat.

"Nah, she'd go with "Local Man Killed." Why mention another city."

She had me there.

Despite Emily, I managed to get a few sentences into the story. In addition to calling Jose well loved in the community, I called him "an important community organizer in lower Manhattan" and mentioned the many appearances he had made in front of Judge Joe Solomon trying to keep the Lower East Side Latino Community Center open. That, of course, meant mentioning His Honor's connection to the mayor. Emily would not let me go beyond that.

The police didn't want to consider those connections either. When they finally did show up at the Center, they went through the motions. They asked a few questions and sifted through some papers, only because Helen insisted they were important. Overall, the whole effort was desultory.

By that time, the police had seven suspects in custody — seven punks from the projects. Two of them had never been arrested before. Two had warrants out on them. The other three had been previously arrested for such *heinous crimes* as pick-pocketing, selling reefer, and public lewdness, which came down to pissing in a vacant lot. The two with arrest warrants hanging over them had a mugging and a breaking and entering in their respective pasts. Put the seven of them together and they certainly didn't equal one murderer.

The seven were all poor. They'd get public defenders if and when the D.A. brought charges. I spent an afternoon calling his office to find out why things were going so slowly.

I was given a runaround.

"Making sure we have an airtight case."

"They're in custody, no rush."

I said something about their right to a speedy trial. The assistant to the Assistant D.A., to whom I was talking, scoffed, "Don't worry. We wouldn't want to violate their precious Constitutional rights."

There was a click and the line went dead.

I got home late that night. Beat, I nuked some canned ravioli and pushed a few barely digestible spoonfuls into my face. Dumping the rest, I left the bowl in the sink. I hoped it would piss my roommates off.

I went to the john, a cigarette hanging from my mouth. Dropping ashes into the bathroom sink, I half-brushed my teeth, took a swig of Scope, and spit.

"Bed," I told myself, exhausted with the effort of walking into my room.

I was too numb to notice it at first.

Pulling off my clothes, I started to lie down. On my pillow was a copy of the paper, my paper, the dumb Elmhurst rag. It was folded. I picked it up, and a tape cassette fell to the floor.

"What the hell?" I got out my Sony and played it. A death threat, a fucking death threat left on my pillow.

The voice was deep, the message was crude, and the words were carefully pronounced except for an "s" added to death and to fuck. The message left no question, I was to stay out of Jose's "deaths" or I would be killed.

"Forget those stories. Stay the fucks out of that Spic's deaths or you're joining him. Those kids are guilty."

Quick, to the point, and terrifying.

It took a few minutes and a few replays before I began to comprehend. I took the tape out of the machine and hid it in a box of oatmeal, not original, but reasonably safe.

Then I did what any sane man would, I called Mo and, I called Julio Martinez, the head of The Latins. I was unsure what Julio would or could do, but I was certain he'd be pissed, which would get some kind of support. Julio surprised me by promising round-the-clock protection. It sounded good for the moment, but …

Like you protected Jose?

I thanked him anyway.

Mo said, "Sit tight. Don't talk about it. Just let me look into it."

No promise, no protection. Still, of the two, I was surer that Mo could and would help. I appreciated the idea of one or two Latins trailing around after me when they could, but Mo was the man with real connections.

Life's about whom you know. No matter if we're talking business, government, or the mob. Maybe in this case all three?

Yeah, this was a case of who knew whom. Why, after all, did the District Attorney go so slowly with seven nobodies? If the cops were so sure, why not just arraign them and let Legal Aid do its thing? I figured the D.A. had to know they weren't guilty. Anyone with half a brain would know that. Clearly, they were stalling. Why?

For the sake of John Hunter? Maybe. If the kids were framed, the case would be closed and the nonexistent investor could take possession of his property. Once he was in possession, would anybody from the Center have standing in court? Probably not. The Alphabet City land grab could go forward without interruption. The moneymaking paperwork could be done before the new buildings came tumbling down.

Another question: how did somebody from this scheme get around to me? How did they know my name? From that dumb watered-down article about Jose's funeral with a phony byline? Not likely. But, somebody, somehow …

Suspicion went into overdrive. The inner dialog went round and round. I kept telling myself I was being paranoid. I kept answering back, "Even paranoids have enemies."

Mo told me to keep quiet. I ignored him. I had to. This shit was real, a real story, a real frame, real guys sitting in jail, and a fucking real threat.

I got the cassette out of the cereal and played it again.

Yeah, fucking real.

There was one thing to do, and it had to be done quickly: make a noise about those punks.

I called a friend, Jim Sergeant, at *The Village News*. Not much of a newspaper. Not much of a reporter, second-stringer at best. But, *The News* billed itself as a crusading, seeker-of-truth in the corrupt jungle of the city, and Jim did have a real byline. I hated to give away any of my story, but those punks were going to sit in jail as long as the Queens District Attorney could keep them there.

"It might be a story," Jim said as he nibbled a piled-high Katz's pastrami on rye. "I'll look into it." A blob of mustard fell onto his tie.

"Jim, this is real. Why else would those kids be rotting?"

"Maybe 'cause they're just unimportant." He was more interested in the stain on his Times-Square-cheap tie than in anything I had to say.

Much as I wanted to frost the cake, I wasn't going to tell him about the death threat. "I think there's more to it," was the best I could do.

If they had to wait for Jim, those kids would be gray before their case would be heard. Then, if they were lucky, they'd end up doing twenty-five in Attica.

I had one last card to play. Not an ace in the hole, more like being an asshole.

I called Dad. I begged and argued. Reluctantly, he agreed to lend me enough money for a lawyer. He probably believed I was the one in trouble and didn't want to admit it.

In a way Dad would have been right—the more I meddled the more danger I'd be in. At least I could smell that Pulitzer.

Just like Woodward and Bernstein.

I told myself that my story was going to make a difference. My grandiose thinking at its best. I was going to take down the man, whoever he was. I was going to keep my word to Maria. I was doing the right thing. It felt good. For once I even knew what the right thing was and I was going to do it.

Maybe it is Jose's influence.

Dad sent me a check for two grand.

I tried Mike Jacobs, the lawyer for the Center.

"I'm a business lawyer, I don't do criminal."

Maybe he was telling the truth; maybe he was scared. He knew a guy in Jamaica who was desperate for work and could maneuver his way around criminal courts.

I knew enough about the legal system to understand that as soon as somebody, a lawyer, was demanding they be arraigned, either the kids would be charged and get free Legal Aid, or the charges would be dropped and they'd be free. Either way, get them a lawyer and something would have to happen. The D.A. wouldn't be able to stall.

Two thousand and all the lawyer got to do is file some papers. Tough work. No wonder the world hates shysters.

Mike Faraday was a redheaded, freckle-faced caricature of a young, inexperienced, Irish lawyer. He looked younger than me with only a hint of a beard and a voice that was still deciding whether to change.

Hardly the image to instill confidence, but Faraday was, according to the Center's attorney, a decent guy who'd do his best. That was what I needed. That was what those seven kids needed.

Faraday was enthusiastic about the case.

For two grand, I would sound enthusiastic, too.

I explained my idea that the kids would end up with legal aide attorneys once they were arraigned, if they were arraigned. That was okay with him.

"Sure, I love making those bastards bleed a little," he replied when I asked if he'd take the case.

The kids or the D.A.?

"I take it you don't care for the system?"

"That's an understatement," Faraday responded. "They're always screwing with little guys."

"How much is this going to cost?"

"Hell, I'd do it for free. How does five hundred sound?"

"Great." I pictured myself returning fifteen hundred to my father.

Maybe twelve fifty. Keep a little for me. He wouldn't know and I could ...

"Each," Faraday added as if it were an afterthought.

Shit!

I did the math. "That's thirty-five hundred."

"Right."

"I don't have that much."

"That might be a problem."

"You were ready to do it for nothing," I said.

"That was just a manner of speaking. You know, to let you know I was enthusiastic. I have to make a living, pay the rent." The sweep of his hand took in his walk-in-closet office.

"Could you make a little less of a living?"

"Let's cut to the chase. What do you have?"

"Two grand."

"You're sure you can't get more."

"I got this from my dad. Not going to ask him for more."

"What about these kids' families?"

"Not a pot in the whole bunch. If they did, they'd already be out. Besides, approaching them? I've already gotten death threats." I didn't mind exaggerating the number.

"Because of this shit?"

"Not to go into the whole story, but yeah, because of this shit." I pulled out my father's check. "Here it is, two thousand. Yes or no?" I was feeling a bit of heat under the collar. I knew the guy was entitled to his pay, but, damn, I wanted to keep some of that money.

"One last little thing." Faraday reached for the check. "Approaching them. You have talked to them, right? These guys authorized you to hire them a lawyer, haven't they?"

"No. I never had a chance to talk with them."

Like the cops would let me. Like the D.A. would allow it. Sure.

"You're kidding."

"No. Why?"

"First, because you have no legal standing, so I'd have none. Second, why haven't you at least satisfied yourself that they need help? That they want the help? Hell. That they aren't happy sitting in their cells?"

"I guess it never occurred to me."

I thought for a moment.

"Besides which, I guess I … shit, I admit it, I'm scared. The last place I want to be is around the cops. Whoever killed Jose. They …"

I almost told him more, but how would that help?

Hell, he'd probably up the price.

He laughed. "Don't become a lawyer."

"No way," I promised. "Could you—"

"Yeah, I'll go see them. You hold onto the cash. If they hire me, you pay two grand. If they don't, you owe me …" He looked at my face, which must have been telling my feelings clear and easy. "Oh, shit, you don't owe me anything. If they don't want a lawyer, I've just wasted my time."

He stood up and reached his hand out. I shook it and was relieved. At least I had done something. At least there was the beginning of a plan. "Thanks."

"I'll call you after I see them."

Faraday called that evening. One of my apartment mates took the message. I was to come back the next day with his money.

"Thank, God," I muttered to myself even while I cursed him for the money.

Chapter 28: Evil Takes Form

I grew up with the great American distrust of lawyers and politicians. They fascinate me the same way that bats and slugs fascinate. Mike Faraday seemed a nice enough fellow, and his firm handshake was reassuring. But, I couldn't shake the uncomfortable feeling I was dealing with a bottom-feeder.

I felt even worse when he didn't have to do much to earn his, my, no, my father's money. Faraday saw the seven bangers who had been arrested, which did take calling in a favor or two. At first he was given a runaround, chasing them through the jail system.

There was a threat of *habeas corpus* accompanied by a mention of his buddy who worked at *The Post*.

"You know," Faraday told me, "for an unimportant case, the D.A.'s office sure was uncomfortable when I mentioned publicity. What do you know that you didn't tell me?"

"Nothing. Just politicians protecting their asses."

He looked at me hard and shrugged his shoulders.

"Anyway, I met with your boys. They wanted something to happen, somebody to do something. So I filed a notice of appearance. Now, let the Public Defender get involved."

True to my plan, the District Attorney's office dropped the charges. No need for complicated maneuvering, filing writs, or court appearances. There had never been a case, just a diversion. Nobody wanted to make fools of themselves. Certainly, nobody wanted to be on the ten o'clock news explaining why a bunch of kids had been arrested without evidence.

I was glad. I was resentful. I felt that same ambivalence when my folks' divorce had gone through. I felt it each time I dropped out of a college class. Hell, I'm ambivalent most of the time. I think shrinks call it neurotic. I could be their poster child.

The two young men with outstanding arrest warrants stayed in jail. Them, I stayed away from. I did go to see the others once they were released from jail. Only one of them had ever heard of Jose Figurés before being arrested.

"We didn't do it, man. I heard he was a nice guy. Tried to help people. Next thing, they say I murdered him. I didn't murder nobody."

I reassured the kid that I knew he was innocent and told him that I had been the one who hired Faraday. I figured that legal bastard had been taking the credit for himself. In fact, he had made my involvement clear.

"Yeah, that lawyer told us. Told the cops, too. Said you was a friend of the guy got killed."

Faraday had made it too clear. This time it wasn't a tape left on my bed, it was a phone call. One of my roomies answered. "Tell that fools he's playing with the wrong peoples."

"Jesus, he was scary, Nick," Jay, my gay roommate reported.

"Did he say anything else?"

"Nope, just that, 'Tell that fools he's playing with the wrong peoples.' That's what he said."

"I asked who he was, and 'click' he's gone."

I got out the hidden cassette and played it for him. "That's him. No question, that's him. What's he talking about?"

"Just a story for the paper."

"Look, I don't want to get my ass kicked just because I'm your roommate."

"Yeah, I know. Not to worry."

Easy for me to say. Whoever this guy is, he isn't going away.

"Well, tell him we don't work with you. Tell him this isn't the paper, that we're just roommates"

Hell, even the paper isn't the paper.

"I'm scared, Nick." The poor guy was shaking.

"I know. I know. I told you, I got it covered."

"Well, you tell him. Please. Nick, I'm really scared.

What do you want me to do about it? Let you suck my thumb? My cock?

I wanted to ease my own anxieties and I wanted to get out of that apartment. I felt like the dust and must of the place was enveloping me. I couldn't breathe. I wished Melinda would take me in … just one more time.

Just for the night, baby.

I wanted to bury myself between her breasts and in her vagina. I wanted to return to the womb, and Melinda's womb would have done just fine. The problem was she was still pissed. At least for once in my life I knew why, what I had done.

When I wasn't immersing myself in the poisonous mud of Jose's death or pursuing the trivial stories that kept me in a meager income, I spent my waking hours tailing Melinda.

Obsessed? Hell, yeah. I want her. I want her. I …

No woman wants to be stalked and no woman wants to be around her stalker. I knew that, but it didn't stop me. I stalked her anyway.

Obsessed? Hell, yeah. I want her. I want her. I ….

Meanwhile, I was wondering if she had lied. Maybe they had broken up, for a while anyway. But, she certainly was not over Mo. They were back at it, hot and heavy. My buddy and the girl I wanted, great combination, and just when I needed them both the most.

If my head needed Melinda for comfort, my body needed Mo and his contacts for security.

I didn't want to talk with him. I hadn't taken his advice. I figured he'd be pissed. Still, I knew I needed to call him. Sailing in dangerous waters, it would be a good idea to have some firepower at the ready. I just kept putting the call off.

I knew things were really hitting the fan when my buddy Frank O'Marra stopped taking my calls. The last thing he said to me had been clear. "You ought to have left them punks alone. Nobody needed to get this can opened again. Now you're on the shit list. So stay the hell away from me. This time I mean it, Nick. Stay the fuck away."

"They were innocent, Frank. They didn't do it."

"Yeah, big deal. Look, I tried to warn you. When you asked about that guy."

"Hunter."

"Yeah, him, that guy. I tried to tell you. But, did you listen? Nick, you're messing in deep shit. Back off."

"Jose was my friend. I want his killers caught."

I could hear him snort. "Don't say I didn't warn you. Okay? When they bash your brains in, don't say Frank O'Marra never told ya."

"Yeah, sure. Thanks," I answered. "At least I can save money not buying you beers."

"Boy, are you a shit head."

I couldn't think of a worthwhile response so I hung up.

Fucking bastards.

I banged my hand against the worn desk. The keyboard jumped. The mouse skittered off the desktop and hung by its cord.

God damned fucking bastards!

Chapter 29: Asking Mo

Three days after Mo found me lying unconscious and had taken me back to our campsite, three days after I had heard the voice of God, I managed to actually get out of my sleeping bag. The sunrise that morning at Machu Picchu was intense, bright, and immediate. I felt it in my soul even more than I sensed it with my eyes. "It's as if the world is beginning," I said to David, who was standing next to me.

"Be careful," he responded, "You're beginning to talk like a poet, or worse, like a rabbi."

"A Hebrew poet?" I suggested good-naturedly.

"For that it isn't enough to feel the world; you have to be as one with it."

"I don't—"

"When your soul goes back to creation, when you are totally connected to all that is divine, when you can feel the first sunrise when He made the world, when you feel in touch with that which is God, then you are a Hebrew poet."

"That's a bit much."

"I know. Try doing it for four thousand years. We Jews really need someone else to take a turn."

"A turn?"

"Yeah, at being the chosen people."

"I guess I'll just stay a goy."

"Well, at least you're our goy." He patted me on the shoulder.

We stood in awe of what ancient man and God had created.

It seemed like those days had been eons before. I wasn't sure how Mo would be feeling towards me, not now, and not here in The Big Apple. I figured he would be a least mildly pissed, what with Melinda and all. But, I also figured I was still his goy. He might want to beat the shit out of me, but I figured he wouldn't let me be ambushed.

I gave into my fear, my terror.

Shit, you said you got my back; so where are you?

I dialed Mo's cell. It went to voicemail. I left a brief message asking him to call me at work. I waited. I waited some more. No call. Every sound in the building was freaking me out. Paranoia was running rampant. I felt completely alone.

I tried to write. It seemed a stupid little article, something about a ladies' tea club that had been meeting weekly for over a hundred years. Now that I think about it, I marvel at such devotion to a minor social ritual. Imagine, war times, influenza outbreaks, snow storms and hurricanes, national and local crises of all kinds, and these women making their tea and cakes, sitting down together, engaging in polite discussion, promising to meet again the following week. Members passing, new members joining, a hundred years of dedication. I can't even remember to get to the dentist with that kind of commitment.

I tried to write, but nothing coherent came. Words bounced around in my head only to splash onto the paper without order. I'd type a few lines into the computer, read them, realize that I had said nothing, then hit delete and start over.

"I had tea at the home of Mrs. Martha Whitehorse last Tuesday."

I must have started the damn thing twenty times when Mo showed up. "I wasn't sure a phone call would be enough." He paused. "Or, for that matter, safe." He hugged me.

I nodded and squeezed him tight. Tears of gratitude and relief flowed down my cheeks and into my mouth. I pulled out a dirty handkerchief and blew my nose.

"That bad?" Mo asked.

All I could do was nod again.

Chapter 30: Revelation

I was thinking a lot about Marcie, not missing her, but wanting to go back to Santiago. I wanted to get as far out of New York as I could. I figured her father could get me a job. I doubted that he or Marcie's mother would want me around, but I figured I could wheedle my way back into their lives. Marcie was that desperate. It was a pathetic fantasy, but one I kept telling myself was perfectly reasonable.

The bottom line: I'm a one-hundred-percent, pure American chicken. I was worried about my health. If you consider my smoking and sexual choices, the idea is pretty funny. I may not be consistent, but I sure as hell didn't want to die. Santiago seemed a safe alternative, certainly safer than the political drama which enveloped me.

Having The Latins and Mo around made me feel a little safer. Mo's new advice didn't.

Having found a lawyer for the seven punks, there was no way that I could make believe I was not involved. Therefore, he said to act as if nothing had been said, as if I had not a fear in the world.

"Look, you've got to go on with the whole Community Center thing. Keep pushing. Find out about Jose's death. Keep … keep Hunter from taking over the property. Keep pushing. Use whatever newspaper connections you got and make more. As long as you're out in the open, you're pretty safe. No one wants to kill a cop or a reporter. It's too damn public. It brings the wrong kind of attention."

I saw a flaw in his logic. "Jose was public."

"Which is why they murdered him in Queens and tried to frame those nobody kids."

I attempted to take his advice. Shaking in my shoes, I put on an act like I didn't have a care in the world and all the time looking around to see who was coming after me, and, just as important, who was watching my back.

Helen, good-old, reliable Helen, whom I had originally discounted because she was too beautiful and maybe too in love with Jose, really came through. She stuck with the Center even after Jose was gone. She kept one step behind David to keep him from turning tail. She hounded the lawyers so they wouldn't give up. Maybe it was her way of keeping faith with Jose, her way of staying true to her love for him.

Now, Helen took me under her wing. She and I were the two people still pushing the good fight. So what if my reason was less noble? My goal was to follow Mo's advice and somehow stay alive by staying public, and, yeah, to get the Pulitzer.

Helen and I were not sleeping together. With Melinda off limits, I wanted to. Helen was beautiful and I was anxious horny all the time. We were, however, spending a lot of time together. I had an additional reason for sticking around her. I hoped whoever was threatening me wouldn't kill two people who were involved with the Center at the same time. That might be too obvious. Like Mo had said, the collective forces who were John Hunter didn't want the glare of publicity.

It was a hot, humid Wednesday evening and Helen and I took the subway up to Queens. The cops had called a meeting, and we wanted to be there.

Somehow, we had kept Jose's murder in public view. Maria had used her local network to get calls made—many, many calls. I managed to get a few bits and pieces into the papers and even onto the radio. Helen had used every political ally of the center until they were all avoiding her calls.

Maybe it had paid off, at least that was what we were hoping. The cops in charge of the case had called this public meeting to discuss their progress. Their progress? As if they were planning to make any. What was more important was that they were stuck with keeping the case open and active. As long as the case was there, Jose Figurés was still alive.

We gathered in a school auditorium. It smelled like every school in memory—the oiled wood smell that never fails to make me feel distantly sick, sick the way I would feel when as a kid I would try to convince my mother to keep me home and she'd refuse. Not a real vomiting sick like I get with the flu or from drinking, but there it was, gnawing at my body and worrying my soul. I probably would have felt that way even if we were not in a school auditorium because it was also the feeling of fear trying to make me run when I knew that I couldn't.

A police sergeant held his hands up to quiet the fairly large crowd. I wondered if he was going to tell us to recite the pledge.

The crowd settled into itself with a low buzz of whispered conversations. "I know you have a lot of questions about Jose Figurés' deaths. Jose Figurés was …"

I'm not sure what followed. A quiver was running up and down my spine. *Holy shit, it's him.*

Helen grabbed my arm. "That voice," she hissed.

"I know. The tape."

I wished my roommate were there. I wondered if he would identify the cop's voice, too.

"Jesus, the cops want to kill you."

"Yeah. Shit. Do you think …?" I stared into her eyes. "They must have killed Jose."

"Oh, my God." She started to cry.

"Quiet down, you guys," demanded a woman sitting near us. Too numb to do anything else, we sat through his speech. I didn't hear a word. Well, actually I did. I kept hearing *deaths, deaths, deaths,* hammering at my brain.

When the meeting was over and the crowd was milling its way out the doors, Helen and I made it to the street. I was surprised, but happy to see a few Latins hanging around. I was even happier when Mo came up to us.

"I thought you'd be here. I wanted to make sure you were okay."

"I'm not," I gasped at him. "That cop, the first one, he's the guy."

"What guy?"

"The guy who called him," Helen answered for me. "Didn't you recognize his voice?"

"Yeah. I just wanted to make sure you did, too."

"Oh, we did," Helen assured him. I was too busy sweating and trying not to barf all over both of them to say anything.

Chapter 31: Burmaste

I knew the enemy. I had known the enemy all along. The trouble was that my enemies were always the people I was supposed to trust: my mother in her preoccupation with my father's infidelity and then her addictions to true love and drugs, my brother with his bullying and teasing, teachers and school administrators preoccupied with control, and now the police.

The world was scary, dark, and difficult. I wanted to be back in the sun of Machu Picchu. Altitude sickness or not, I wanted to be in the clean air of The Andes. I would have settled for a cafe or wine bar in Santiago. I might have even considered a campground in the middle of America or puking on the streets in Oregon. I wanted to be somewhere, anywhere … anywhere but New York City.

There was something else I wanted. I wanted that Pulitzer. Wanting is easy. Getting what you want is always another thing. The story was right there. It was going to be my big break, my prize. Terrified as I was, I hadn't lost the dream.

The man, or men, who were making believe that John Hunter existed, that he was a real person, were pushing to get into the Center. The cranes were still swinging, the great iron balls were still bombarding the age-beaten walkups of Alphabet City, the old buildings were still swaying and ready to topple if they were not leaning one against the other for support. The high-rises were now going up even while, slowly but perceptibly, the new structures were sinking into the silt and sand. The economy was strong, and the city's real estate market was booming. Only the piercing shrill voice of Jose's ghost was in the way. The exorcism was supposed to be simple. The mysterious Hunter would take possession and then he would probably sell the building off to one of the developers. They would have to pay extra, but they'd build there, too. The architectural plans had already been approved. No sense waiting for a little thing like the law to take its course.

Still, we held on. The longer David, Helen, I, and the Latino community held, the more attention the media was paying. There were exposés, only a few at first. Then came the first reports of major structural problems. Banks were hesitating with their loans. Reporters were starting to quote Helen and even me; they were asking for interviews.

I had become the de facto press secretary for the Center. I didn't much care for the job. I wanted to be writing breaking stories. Instead, I was providing background for other reporters. One thing, I wasn't telling them about the police involvement in Jose's murder. That was a story I was keeping for myself. I figured it was going to be the big one. For the rest of the world it was an unsolved random act of violence.

And, I certainly wasn't going to mention my trip to Washington. That was between Mo and me. It was dangerous territory and who knew what dragons roamed that sea?

When a large ship turns, it takes time and distance. Inertia keeps it moving in the original direction. The same thing was happening right in front of me. Gradually, the bank loans dried up, the Mannlich trucks and heavy equipment disappeared from the streets, the wrecking slowed, and construction projects ground to a finish while no new ones started.

The city announced a number of renewal and road construction projects, many of them projects that had long been on hold because there wasn't enough money. Most of the projects were needed, but the mayor's office had no explanation of why the sudden burst of spending.

No one was shocked when the same companies that had been destroying Alphabet City received the new contracts. Mannlich Construction, the destroyers of that first earth-shaking morning, received some of the biggest contracts. A payoff for their cooperation? No one could prove it, but those companies were heavily invested in the slowly sinking buildings, some that would never be completed and others that would never be used, certainly never sold as co-ops and condos to the middle class.

Alphabet City had become old news. I wasn't happy about the change. I still had the story of Jose's murder to write. I figured it soon would no longer be of interest. My opportunity might pass untaken.

A part of me was happy to have it over.

Maybe I'm not cut out to be a reporter.

That thought often passed through my head as I sat in Queens writing journalistic drivel.

I wrote a special piece about school lunch ladies. Emily was delighted.

Maybe I'm not cut out to be a reporter.

One of the local churches was going ecumenical; they were going to share space with other denominations. Another big story by my editor's standards.

Maybe I'm not cut out to be a reporter.

At least Hunter will go back into his government hole. There's no point in his pushing to get control of that old school now.

Eventually the man we knew as Hunter came by the center to talk at David and Helen. I happened to be there. We were trying to organize yet one more rally to raise money, perhaps to save the Center or at least to save its programs. I was supposed to write a press release.

I hung at the coffee pot and chatted up one of the volunteers, a not so pretty, young woman whose long black hair needed a good wash and set. It was just that Melinda was around, and I was trying—hoping—to make her jealous.

Despite the difference in height, Hunter, his eyes made predatory by those thick glasses, got right in David's face and made it clear he wasn't letting go of the building no matter what else happened. "I don't do failure," he shouted, "and I want my building."

David, with Helen physically pushing to keep him from backing away, tried to respond. "What if we can raise the money and buy it from you?"

Hunter sneered. "And let you win? That isn't happening."

Why so much steam?

It wasn't like the inevitable could be stopped. The sinkhole of Alphabet City was opening up and he, or his handlers, should have been smart enough to walk away. What the hell were a few million bucks when you're playing with Uncle Sam's money?

If we can raise the money? Why not just take it? What's wrong with this guy?

Burmaste was with him. That was a surprise. The bulky Cuban asked for me, which was downright odd. We had never met, but I had seen Burmaste, not just in newspapers and on the tube, but also in living, breathing, snowy life. He looked like smarmy death, dressed up in expensive low-taste clothes with a look of artificial tan and perfectly groomed contempt.

He came up really close to me like he was trying to intimidate me and whispered, his voice a hoarse imitation of a gangster movie, "We should talk."

I stepped back. "Sure. How's your golf game?"

"Don't be a wise-ass."

"I take it you don't play golf?"

"Look, you're a walking dead man. Understand me? You *will* get yours." His voice uncoiled like a snake striking. "You just couldn't keep your stupid-ass nose out of things that didn't concern you."

"I'm a reporter, and I found a story, a goddamn great story." I said it and, for the moment, even believed it.

"Reporter," he snarled. "Hell, you're Little League."

"Not after I nail you and Hunter and a few other phonies."

He laughed. "The only nailing will be your coffin. Figurés is dead. And you'll be, too."

"By a cop no doubt." I tried to say it casually and I watched for the reaction.

Burmaste did not disappoint. Almost jumping away from me, he pulled a big, checker-boarded handkerchief from his breast pocket and blew his nose twice. I knew it was to give himself time. I had seen him use the same method before. Of course that had been on TV. It was a well-practiced ploy.

I responded with a smart-assed grin.

"You may think you know things, and you may think you're cool, but I promise you're going to pay. You are a dead man."

I couldn't resist. "Is that what you talked about in Maryland?"

This time Burmaste made no effort to mask his reaction. "You are fucking dead." He spit the words at me.

"I'm really scared." I said it in what I hoped sounded like a mocking tone. All the while I knew it was true. I could feel myself shaking.

"Fuck you." The sneer in his voice was at odds with the discomfort I saw in his eyes. For the first time I realized that he was as scared as I. I just didn't know why.

Maybe I could prove the cops killed Jose. Maybe I could prove Burmaste had some sort of tie to the C.I.A. What I couldn't prove was that the bastard had ordered Jose's death. I really couldn't touch him, so why the hell was he so worried?

Mo had no clue either, at least not that he was going to share with me. We met that night at our new rendezvous, Cookie's, a diner in Brooklyn. It was a place where nobody in his or her right mind would eat. In fact, even I was grossed out sitting on sticky Naugahyde looking at the stained, chipped green Formica tabletop. The table was so discolored that it looked like somebody had vomited. We met at Cookie's because Mo figured nobody would ever see us there, at least nobody who was sober.

We ordered coffee and made believe we were drinking it. The coffee's boiled again-and-again fumes attacked my eyes and nose. I'm not the squeamish type, not about cleanliness, and I love strong coffee, but I would rather have drunk right out of The East River.

"Something's going on that's bigger than Jose," Mo said.

"But I don't know what."

"They don't know what you do or don't know. They just know you're dangerous." Mo dumped some sugar into his cup and unconsciously swirled it.

"Who are the fucking *they*?"

"People you don't want to know."

"Hell, I don't want to know Burmaste, but I do."

"He's the least of your worries."

"Great."

What does that mean?

We sat and looked at each other for a couple of minutes. I felt stupid. My hands folded in front of me like a kid in school. Finally, I asked the question that had been rattling around in my mind. "Mo, could you get me out of the country?"

"Where?"

"I have no idea. Maybe back to Chile? Maybe to Peru?"

"Do you think you'd be safe there?"

"What do you … yeah, they wouldn't … I don't know."

He laughed at my discomfort. "Nick, you're playing in the Big Leagues now."

"How do I get dropped back down to the Minors?"

"You don't. One thing I can guarantee you: you try to hide, and they'll come after you. You're safest here, at least for now. Just—"

"I know," I interrupted, "just act like I'm not scared and keep in public places. But for how long?"

"Until it's over." He smiled enigmatically, looked at the check, put a few bills on the table, and made for the door. I watched his gray sports coat recede into the night until he had blended into the shadows.

I waited five minutes. That was standard procedure. Mo would leave, and I would give him time to get clear of me. I knew that somewhere outside Cookie's there would be one of the Latin's and maybe even a *Mossad* agent waiting to follow me back to the apartment.

Deciding that Mo had over-tipped, I picked up two singles and stuffed them into my pocket. "Good night," I called out to the waitress. While she looked my way, I pulled one of those singles back out and dropped it onto the table.

Chapter 32: Follow the Benjamins

"Follow the money."

"Huh?"

"Isn't that what Deep Throat was about?"

I didn't usually bother listening. Jay mooned over me the way I obsessed about Melinda and Sue. Experimenting had been a mistake, not because it hadn't felt good, but because it had turned him on. When he talked, everything was laced with innuendos.

I had forgotten it, but besides being into men, Jay was also into bookkeeping. He was a buttoned-down accounting major. Dressed in a light grey suit with blue shirt and a conservative tie, my roomy was big bank material.

"What does a sex movie have to do with anything?"

"Not the sex thing, the other Deep Throat. The one who … you know, Nixon and those two reporters."

"Woodward and Bernstein""

"Yeah, them. Didn't he tell them?"

"Tell them what?"

"Follow the money, Nick. Follow the money."

"What money?"

"Who's getting rich in Alphabet City? Follow the money."

Jay's words made sense.

Why have I not thought of that? Why has Mo missed it?

I didn't know who was getting rich, not who all the players were, but I did know one thing. Every time I turned around down there, I saw another Mannlich Construction truck, crane, cement mixer. A place to begin looking for the Benjamins.

Who the hell is Mannlich and what does he have to do with Jose?

"You may be right, Jay."

"Hey, where you going?"

I was almost out the door.

"City Hall." It blew my mind, but I needed to see papers, follow the corporate trail.

"What about me?"

"You?"

"Don't I get to be Deep Throat?"

"Not now, Jay. Maybe another time."

I called Helen. She was better at finding out paperwork things than I. She met me at the corporation's office.

Mannlich Construction: A privately held corporation, headquartered in New York City, specializing in heavy equipment and construction. Incorporated nineteen ninety-five. There was no Mannlich, just the name of the company, made up just like that mountain logo. There were names, some I expected and some that confused. Anthony Puglese was president and CEO. His son John vice-president and CFO. And there they were, the major stockholders, among them: the mayor, Burmaste, the Chief of Detectives, John Hunter, a guy I knew didn't exist, even Judge Joe Solomon.

A trail of Benjamins tying City Hall, the police, the courts, the mob, and some shadow part of the federal government. For all the answers, I was still swimming in questions. Who the fuck was John Hunter? Why was he the one to buy the school? What did Mannlich have to do with Washington? What the hell was going on?

And of course, if they find out what I know, will they bash my head in, too?

Chapter 33: Night Crawler

Nighttime is for prowling. Just ask a cat, a burglar, a druggie, or a pervert. I guess I fall into the last group. When anxiety hits the hardest, I wander the streets looking for something to take care of that sharp, peeling edge. Sometimes it's been a hooker, sometimes a peep show, once in a while when I've been lucky there has been a girlfriend. To be honest, even when I've had girlfriends I've prowled. I dumped Estrella. I cheated on Marcie. I cheated on Melinda.

Love is wonderful, but instinct rules.

Santiago, New York City and everywhere in between, it never mattered. When the urge hit, I turned into a stalker, a tom with nothing but heat on his mind. Especially when scared and confused, the urge takes possession of the body and leaves the head behind. The fact is fear, real gut-level fear, has always helped to bring on that urge. I've known lots of guys who jerked off when anxious. I certainly won't pretend I'm not one of them. But, masturbation sometimes, many times, is just not enough.

That night, terrified, confused, and excitedly wondering if Mannlich Construction might offer the answers to a bunch of questions and the beginning of a bunch more, there was no way I was going to sleep.

I didn't want anyone watching me while I crept around the city — not The Latins or Mo and the Mossad, and certainly not Burmaste's friends in blue. I was never sure which, if any, of them would be waiting in the Brooklyn streets outside the apartment I shared.

I was scared. It didn't make any difference. I was going out to find some ass, and I was determined to not be seen.

I've always been good at sneaking, kind of a stealth person floating just below the radar whenever I could. I honed those skills while Dad was chasing his girlfriends and I was supposedly going to middle and high school. Weed in the woods had become my better alternative to classes. Most of the time, teachers didn't know, or perhaps didn't care, that I was absent. They took attendance, but they never seemed to notice if the super-quiet kid in the heavy-metal clothes who sat in the back of the classroom was there or not. Only when grades came out did anyone notice the extent of my missed tests and homeworks. By then, too late to make up the work or offer extra credit assignments, most teachers just gave me a minimal pass rather than explain why they hadn't noticed the negative space I inhabited.

I hoped my cloak of invisibility would work again. Putting on my ratty, go-to-the-peepshow clothes, I slouched down the stairs and into the Brooklyn night. It was dark, at least by New York standards, only a crescent moon and many of the streetlights were out. A guy slumped against one of the dead lights. I went the other way. Halfway down the block I slipped into a doorway and watched to see if he followed. He did in a half-drunken wobble. Was it real or shammed? I ran, turned a corner, went half a block, and hid again. The son of a bitch shambled around the corner. Had he picked up speed? Maybe invisibility wasn't my strong suit after all. I slipped out of concealment and, hugging buildings and crouching next to stoops to catch my breath, I made it to the next corner and ran again. I circled the block and waited in the doorway of the apartment house next to mine. I waited for a while, but the guy didn't reappear. Had I given him the slip or was he simply a harmless drunk? I didn't care. I didn't want to know. I headed out; the peep shows called.

I tried to walk in shadows as I made my way to the nearest subway. When I got there, the same drunk was holding up another damn lamppost.

I saw him and prayed that he didn't see me. I slipped away and took off for the next station down the line. I ran for a bit. The effort, the anxiety, and lifestyle of sloth and heavy tobacco use pretty well did me in. I felt like I was going to have a heart attack. I switched to an unsteady walk.

I went into an all-night donut shop, half fell onto a stool, and ordered coffee and a French crueler. I ordered it from the air, assuming one of the two workers would respond. I didn't realize that I was suddenly again invisible.

After giving me enough time to cool my heels and get my breath back, one of the workers behind the counter came over and asked what I wanted. He made it clear that my earlier order had been totally ignored, so I said it again, adding a slightly sarcastic please. He was an acne-scarred, geeky guy. The other server, a girl, was kind of decent looking with thin, stringy hair, and a pieced lip.

I wouldn't mind putting her thumb in my coffee.

The waitress busily ignored me. Maybe I had become half visible, the wrong half.

I hung at the donut shop and watched the late-nighters. They were a motley collection: workers coming and going to and from their shifts, drunks trying to sober up before going home to their spouses and a few with no homes to go to, students cramming for exams, young couples without money making believe that they were having good time dates. Some were downright loquacious, others barely said a word. Some brought books and read. A few bought newspapers from the box just outside and perused the employment ads. Bodies hunched with inevitability and strain. Faces pasty and stressed. No one happy. An all-night donut shop isn't the place for bluebirds.

Eventually, Pimple Face came back and asked if I wanted more coffee. "Only seventy-five cents. With another donut only fifty."

"Thanks, but no thanks." My welcome had worn thin. "I guess it's time to get going."

"Yeah. Have a good night."

"You, too." I paid and left a quarter next to my empty cup.

For Clearasil.

I headed for my favorite peep, wishing, hoping that Droopy-Assed Sue had magically returned. I thought about Baltimore and I missed her. I wanted a familiar face, someone I knew to cross my path. Maybe, just maybe, I really wanted it to be her.

Weird, I want to be invisible and then I want to be around someone, not just anyone, but somebody I have feelings about. I know. I guess I'm just one of those good old neurotics.

I chuckled. Then, spooked.

Shit! Maybe somebody does know me.

I whirled around to check. No one in sight. I took off running. The next block I slowed down. Panting and holding my side, I kept walking towards the subway, continuing towards debauchery.

Chapter 34: Morning After

The phone intruded into my dreams. One moment I was trapped on a strange planet with a group of sexy women. I, the one male and their leader, was trying to guide them to freedom from the clutches of crafty, shape-changing natives. The labyrinth of escape involved subterfuge, careful thinking, and rapid, strong physicality. The women, bright-eyed and eager, followed without question.

It had started out the dream of a hero. Then there was a fire alarm, and I was fleeing. No longer the hero, I was in the vanguard of the fearful. I was running for my life, and terror held my heart in its powerful hands. I fought my way through the smoke and cinders that swirled around my fright and woke to Mo's call.

"You enjoy the peep show?" Mo's question threw me even more than the fact that he had called at seven in the morning.

I was hung over, in need of more sleep, and aching to return to my heroic dream.

"What?" I tasted the foulness of the night before.

When did I last brush my teeth?

If that moment was any indicator, it had probably been months.

"I asked how the peep show was." Mo kept his voice steady, without a hint of sarcasm or judgment. His control made me angry, no, furious. Visions of Melinda crashed into my eyeballs. It took a moment to get control, bare control.

"Hey, are you there?" he asked.

"Yeah, sure. It was okay, I guess. Nothing I haven't seen before."

"I'm sure." He took a breath. "It wasn't too smart."

"I know, but I wasn't thinking. I guess I was in a rut."

"The head of a penis—"

"What?"

"The head of a penis, it got no brain."

"Oh, yeah."

Subtle. Fuck you, Mo.

"Luckily my man was able to follow you."

"The guy hanging on the lamppost?"

"No. Not him. I don't know if that guy was watching you or just another drunk in the night. You never saw my guy."

"He must be good."

"The best. But, he's kind of pissed at you."

"I can understand—"

"Look, I want you to let me know."

There was silence.

Maybe I should play dumb. He already thinks I'm a stupid shit. Maybe dumb will get me some slack.

It was a technique that had always worked in school. "Let you know what?"

"Don't play dumb. Let me know when you're going out, and use the regular apartment phone to do it and call me on my business phone."

"Don't you think they have a tap on those phones?"

"Sure. At least on yours. That's the point. They'll know where you're going, but they'll also know that we've got your back."

"Great plan." I stopped with the next words already on my tongue. I stopped to consider them. "Of course that makes me great bait—using your chum as chum or is it chump?"

"Nick, I don't want to catch them in the act of killing you. What good would that do anybody? I couldn't even come forward."

"Why not?"

"For obvious reasons that we won't discuss on the phone, not even this one."

"So what could you do?"

"Protect you."

No need for Mo to say more. "Look, man, sorry I gave your guy a hard time. I know it was kind of stupid, but I really wanted, no I needed to get the hell out of here."

"Fine. I understand. Just, look, don't do that dumb spy routine again. Okay? Okay?"

"Yeah, sure. I promise. Tell your guy I'm sorry."

"Yeah, I'll do that." Mo's tone made it obvious he had no such intention.

"I really am sorry."

"Just keep your sorry butt in sight."

"I get the message, but for how long?" My voice whined its way through my nasal cavities.

"Until it's safe. Until you're safe."

"I know, but when?"

"We'll talk about that later." I could feel the words spit out of his mouth and into the prepaid, untraceable cell phone that he had dedicated to my protection, a mate to the one he had given me, the one I usually used to call him. I could sense his frustration race across the void to some satellite held in space by forces that I could not comprehend and shot back to earth, forcing their way through telephone lines beneath the streets, and finally, after that incredible journey, boxing my ear with his irritation.

I was overwhelmed by all that I could not understand.

"Yeah, later, man," I answered meekly. The phone went dead.

At least you can't slam the receiver down on a cell phone.

I felt like shit. My head wanted to explode and my guts wanted to heave. It was not just the night before. It was not being jolted out of my dream. It was not a lack of sleep. It was the toll of friends whom I had lost or was losing. Marcie, Melinda, Frank, now possibly Mo, and most of all, Jose. I sat in a dilapidated green and gold chair. One of my roommates' families had contributed it to our furniture collective. It smelled of must and cat piss. The smell matched my depression and loneliness; it garnished the emptiness of my life. With nothing else to do, I sat and brooded, stared at faded wallpaper and thought.

I thought about Melinda and about Marcie. Then about Estrella, visualizing her: the beautiful lime of her eyes filled with tears, tears I had caused. Suddenly, it was all too real, too painful. Estrella had been special, caring. And I, wrapped in myself, had not appreciated.

The darkness of my thoughts turned back to Jose. I imagined him sitting at his cluttered desk in the Center, his jaw set with determination, his fingers drumming the desktop. "I gotta tell ya, Nick …" What did I want him to say? What did I want him to tell me?

Jose dead, killed for fighting, killed for caring.

I thought about droopy-assed Sue and her strange vulnerability. I remembered the relief I found in her body that terrified night in Baltimore.

Peru. The old man with his pan flute. His music in my head. The sound eased my pain, not just the pain of my hangover and my embarrassment, but more importantly, the pain of my soul.

Chapter 35: That Day

It had not been a special day. It hadn't been an ordinary day. It was the day Mom left us.

We waited for the bus. Winter was coming. Leaves cluttered the gutters. Geese formed in great Vs and flew in sweeping circles overhead.

Tommy Grasso from down the street was talking about the circus. Did I want to go? Had I gone? Something about tigers? My brother Jim was saying Mom wouldn't let me because they'd keep me for the freak show.

"You're the freak," I whined, filled with childish rage which brought a sadistic chuckle from Jim.

Mom, suddenly there and bent to our eye level, held the front of my windbreaker in her left hand and my brother's in her right. He pulled against her grip, and she yelled, "Stop squirming."

Jim pulled again and then surrendered.

I stood mute, waiting and wondering.

"I won't be here when you get home from school."

"Where are you going?" my brother asked.

"Can I come?" I asked.

"Away."

"To the hospital? Is your head bad again?" Jim's voice filled with tears.

"No. I'm fine. I am very, very fine. Better then fine. I've found a man whom I love and who loves me. He has a houseboat in Key West. We're going to live there. Vacation you'll come and visit. You can sleep on the houseboat and go fishing and swimming. It will be wonderful."

"Where is Key West?" I asked. "Can we come with you?"

"It's in Mexico," my brother answered. "Besides, we got school."

"Florida," Mom said.

"Does Dad know?" My brother was older, more practical, more aware of her problems.

"Not yet. I'll call him. I'm sure he'll have Mrs. Gladstone here when you get home. I am sure he'll—"

"Yeah," my brother interrupted. "He's done it lots of times." Jim twisted to free his jacket from her grasp.

"When will you be back?" I asked fighting back tears.

Mom released my windbreaker and mussed my hair. "I won't be back, Nicky. I told you, I love Paul and he loves me. We'll be living in Key West. Mrs. Gladstone—"

The bus pulled up. My brother, finally free, pulled away and stormed up the bus stairs. "Come on, Nick!"

I followed him.

We were into the next block before I realized Mom had not said she loved us—had not said she loved me. The tears flowed.

"Baby," Jim hissed at me loudly enough to draw attention.

I sobbed, and my big brother slapped the back of my head in derision.

That afternoon, Mrs. Gladstone was there. It was an old routine practiced during Mom's stays in the hospital: Mrs. Gladstone, the cleaning ladies, Dad getting home earlier and leaving later, Dad being happier.

"Do you miss her?" my brother asked one morning when the three of us were eating Cheerios.

"Who?" Dad asked. "You want more milk?"

"Mom."

"Oh. No." He poured milk into our glasses.

I said nothing. Instead, I again helplessly fought tears.

Chapter 36: Afterlife

After the Washington adventure and the highs and lows it evoked, after the excitement and terror of playing the secret agent, after the anxiety-driven sexual need, after all that had subsided, my life descended into its own rut. Days came and went in meaningless succession. Mired in my job, I managed to keep my head above the quicksand of termination. There were no more big stories to chase, no more cloak-and-dagger trips to Washington. There was, instead, a steady stream of trivia. Bridge clubs gave way to Little League, which in turn became school honor roles, and always those seemingly all-important school lunch menus. What exciting lives the people of Elmhurst were living. If I was writing about a boring world, the one in which I personally lived was mind-numbing.

Even the vestiges of the Community Center were gone. David had moved on; I had no idea to where. Melinda, whose relationship with Mo had ended as unceremoniously as it had begun, had taken a job at a private nursery school and hooked-up with a commodities broker. His office was high in the World Trade Center. Perhaps it was symbolic. Melinda was giving up her "save the world" phase and drifting back to her family's wealthy roots.

Helen had boxed the important papers from the Center and given them to Maria, then, she, too, drifted away. Finding a new cause and presumably a new leader to whom she could devote herself.

Maria mourned until she met Diego.

After all those years of lonely weeknights, she'll have someone there.

I couldn't begrudge Maria that comfort.

They were soon to be married. I didn't expect to be invited to the wedding. I wondered if he smoked cigarillos.

Presumably, the non-existent John Hunter got his money back from the city because the building remained an abandoned school, covered in angry graffiti. That wasn't surprising since development in Alphabet City slowed to its pre-boom, pre-scam trickle.

The first lawsuits over faulty construction made their appearance in the courts and the back pages of newspapers, newspapers that hadn't been interested in what I had to say. Newspapers for which I had hoped to work and which now seemed impossibly inaccessible.

My protective guard melted away. Julio told me The Latins could no longer waste time protecting me, but that I could call him if anything happened or if I knew that I was going into a dangerous situation. I knew it wasn't so much about my being safe, or their wasting time, as it was that their way of life and their remaining homes were again protected by the apathy of government. There was no longer an advantage in driving the gang from Alphabet City, no money to be made by redevelopment.

The Latin's defection was okay with me. In my mind I had always been relying on Mo. I knew no matter how pissed he might get that he would never just hang me out. That was true enough, but he eventually told me he thought the danger had passed. At least he told me in person.

We occasionally got together for coffee, usually in one of the dives he considered safe, sometimes in the nicer place that I had come to understand his "company" ran. The meetings were short and to the point. I don't think it was because of my night of sneaking off to carouse, or the other nights when I had called to tell him of my primitive needs before leaving the apartment. I think he was simply tired of the shallowness of my life, of my pathetic expectation that one day the big story would plunk itself down in front of me.

"The world isn't that simple," Mo had said to me one night over coffee.

I responded that I already knew this wondrous piece of news. Deep inside, I questioned if I really was up to dealing with the world's complexities.

If I had become more to Emily's editorial liking, I had certainly lost the drive to be better. Perhaps Emily was right that I should stick to the simple stuff like school lunches and library programs.

Being a reporter had seemed exciting, sexy, and easy. That had been when I was a kid in high school. But I was no longer a kid, just a lonely, insecure, and increasingly bitter, chain-smoking, caffeine-addicted guy slouching his way through life.

I was also horny, but what else was new? Anxiety turned my prick head on. Boredom did the same thing.

I was horny and I was once again obsessed, obsessed with lard-assed Sue. No good reason. That's the way I am. I get an idea and it takes over. Our night in Baltimore had taken on the allure of romance. I told myself that I was in love. I started haunting the peeps and the strip joints in the hope I would again find her.

There were plenty of other women available, not for relationships, but certainly for sex, or for just watching. Plenty of them were even good lookers, girls I might in the past have drooled over. But I just had one woman on my mind, one droopy-assed, big-busted woman with light lime-green eyes. One woman whom I had watched in New York and screwed in Baltimore.

At least Sue gave me something to think about. She took the place of Jose, his murder, John Hunter, Mo, Melinda, and my job, especially my job. I knew how to do it by then. I could write the damn stupid articles my boss wanted in my fucking sleep. I followed her formats, and she was happy and gave me more assignments and a small raise. They would never win me a Pulitzer or even a better job, but they kept my bills paid, and I didn't have to ask Dad for more money.

The ranks of the hookers around Times Square had been thinned by police harassment. I loved the irony: an administration, which I saw as totally without scruples, and a police department willing to provide the city administration with murderers on demand, were combined in efforts to rid the streets of New York of one of their great and most colorful attractions and a source of modest pleasure for visitors and locals alike.

Sure, sex crimes involve abuse to women and that's wrong. And, there are STDs galore, to say nothing of crabs.

Still, it is, as they say, a hard knock life; and most hookers can't survive without doing flat work. That's how it is. That's how it has always been. No free pieces of the pie.

Yeah, I'm a consumer, a john. There are plenty of people who'd condemn me for my proclivities. Fuck them. I just liked to get laid by a pro.

I wasn't the first john to get obsessed with a whore or a dancer. I wouldn't be the last.

I did what compulsion demanded; I searched for my big assed Madonna. I didn't find her, but I enjoyed the looking. I certainly wasn't planning on quitting any more than I was quitting screwing.

In this life we do what we gotta do. Bada-bing Bada-boom.

Summer had come, hot and sticky. The heat and humidity settled into the canyons of Manhattan. Lethargy filled the streets of Queens. I wrote stories about kids playing ball, the conditions at municipal swimming pools, and people who gardened in their backyards and met in libraries to talk about their azaleas. Like other working-stiff New Yorkers, I dreamed of getting out of town and settled for an occasional day at Coney Island.

Once a week I hit the local precinct to copy the blotter. I made it a point to avoid Frank. I kept my head down and hoped that I wouldn't be shot. None of the cops talked to me. I didn't want to talk to them. Still, it was as close as I was ever going to come to real reporting.

Mine was a phantom existence, a gray poltergeist roaming the netherworld of the city. I might as well have been dead. I was just too afraid to take a chance on dying. Sometimes it's the fear that keeps a guy from living.

The humid summer was still fighting for survival, but there was an autumnal feel in the occasional breeze. The leaves in Central Park were still green, but I sensed a brittleness to them. Perhaps it was the primordial realization that they weren't long for this world.

Labor Day had just passed. Children were back in school. The endlessly repetitive school lunch menus were back on my assignment sheet. The world was turning without changing. My dreary half-lived life went on.

Mo phoned me at the paper and told me to meet him that evening. We weren't seeing much of each other, usually once every three or four weeks—always at his initiative. At each meeting it was clear he didn't particularly want to be there. Still, Mo was unwilling to drop me, although I was sure he thought I deserved it.

I never called Mo. I had his phone number but was too embarrassed to use it.

Having met only ten nights earlier, I hadn't expected to hear from him for at least another two weeks, maybe longer. And, certainly not at the paper. He never called the paper.

We agreed on a Starbucks near his apartment. I headed back to Brooklyn to get cleaned up. At least shame made me more aware of my appearance when I was around him.

It seemed impossible but, overall, I had managed to become more disheveled and less hygienic. Perhaps it was an expression of my deepening depression. Mo tried to ignore the deterioration at first. Eventually he had said something. So, when we got together, I made an effort, even if it was to shower, scrape a disposable razor across my face and put on a different set of unwashed clothes.

Mo was sitting at a table near the door of the Starbucks when I arrived. He looked harried, a man with too many things on his mind and even more on his plate. There was another man with him, someone I vaguely recognized, but couldn't place. As I approached, the other guy got up and hurriedly left.

"Who is your friendly friend?"

"Somebody who doesn't approve of my meeting you."

"That sounds ominous."

I started to sit down.

"Get yourself some coffee," Mo hissed. "I don't want to be too conspicuous."

I complied even though it sounded ludicrous. In a yuppie-filled Starbucks redolent with that unique smell of burnt coffee, I looked like the neighborhood derelict. Nothing was going to make us inconspicuous.

I ordered a latte and waited for it. I never drank lattes. In fact, I never put milk in my coffee at all, but I felt like I was playing some stupid role. I figured I might as well play it to the hilt. It seemed like forever before I returned to the table.

"Something the matter?" I asked as soon as I sat down.

"I'm leaving."

"I just got here."

"I don't mean Starbucks. I'm leaving the city ... actually the country."

"When?"

"Tonight."

"That's kind of sudden. Where are you going?"

"Home. My assignment here is finished."

"Your assignment?"

"Yeah. She left last night. In the middle of the night she ...." He stopped himself.

"I don't ... Mo, what are you talking about? What assignment?"

"Remember when you went down to Washington?"

"Of course. How could I forget?"

"Remember this?" He pulled one of the photographs I had taken showing the Arab and Burmaste together and slipped it across the table for me to see. I barely had time to focus before he pulled it back and put it in his pocket.

"Yeah. I remember. The snow was—"

"Stay with me, man," he ordered. "The Arab—"

"What about him?"

"He's a half-brother of the woman I've been keeping under surveillance."

"The one who took off last night?"

"Right."

"What does that mean?"

"I'm not sure, but I think it means an attack."

"An attack?" I echoed, my voice raised above discretion.

He shushed me.

"An attack?" I repeated.

What the hell is he talking about?

"I, we, figure that they're planning some kind of attack, another attack on New York, down here, lower Manhattan, maybe the Trade Center again. It must be coming soon or she wouldn't have just disappeared that way."

"Have you told the government?"

"Mine or yours?"

"Either. Both. Hell, I don't know!"

"Of course I have."

"Which?"

"Both. I cabled Jerusalem, and I met with somebody from your CIA."

"Good. I guess."

What does he want me to do?

"Not really. I'm not sure that CIA schnook wanted to know anything. Or …" He paused for a moment, took a sip of coffee, and continued "What the hell. I'm not sure that he didn't already know."

"Didn't know what?"

"Whatever it was that needed to be known."

I was feeling pretty damned dense. I stared blankly at my friend. Conversations and background music murmured around us.

Mo smiled slightly. I smiled back, reflexively, the white noise of the background suddenly oppressive, almost painful.

"The point is," Mo put his hand on my arm to emphasize what he was saying, "you're in danger."

"Me? Why? A nobody. The story is dead. What do I matter?"

"Jose," he hissed. "You know about Jose."

"Nobody remembers Jose."

He grimaced. "You're carrying around some dangerous information."

"About what?"

"About what's going to happen."

"Stop talking in riddles."

"That's how it is, a riddle. Somehow you've ended up in the middle of a riddle, a dangerous riddle."

"What should I do? Go to the government?" I meant it facetiously.

"That might be the worst thing. If I were you, I'd take off. Get out of the country."

"I thought—"

"That was then. This is now. Get the hell out."

"No way I can do that."

"At least get out of New York."

"Where should I go?"

"Far. Some small town far from here." He started to rise. "And, do it now. Don't wait."

Mo was standing. I started to stand, too. He put his hand on my shoulder and pushed me down. "Let me leave first," he whispered. He shook my hand, holding it for an extra second or two. "I don't think we'll ever get to speak again."

"What about emails?"

"No." He stared at me intently. "I don't know what's coming down, but get out of here. And stay the hell away from this part of the city. Something nasty is going to happen around here. So ... just stay away."

"What about you?"

"I told you, I'm out of here."

"Will I ever hear from you again?"

"I don't know." He paused and looked at me with what I supposed was concern and even friendship. "Probably not, but perhaps ... someday ... who knows?"

He walked away.

What about Dad? What should I tell him?

I wanted to call Mo back and demand answers. Answers, what a concept, does anyone ever really have answers?

I watched Mo walk out of the coffee shop and into the gorgeous autumn weather. I always thought New York was at its grandest in the fall.

Chapter 38: After the Dark

Nausea was the only response my mind had been able to formulate, one huge outpouring from my guts and soul. I watched in revulsion and disbelief, looked down to puke, and refocused my eyes on the horror.

Mo had been correct. The next morning the beauty of New York's fall was violated. I was there despite, and because of, Mo's admonition. I had never liked being told "no," and I was not going to start listening that morning.

Besides, there was something in my brain.

There's a story. There has got to be a story. Get there and cover the story.

Despite fear, the sense of coming danger impelled me towards Lower Manhattan. In the singular, I may be a coward, but when the menace is more general, I don't think about it. At least that morning I didn't.

I was up early. Grabbing a cup of coffee and a *Times* from the newsstand near the apartment, I was on the subway by seven-fifteen. Whatever it was, something was driving me toward the financial district, towards Lower Manhattan. It propelled me with the same implacable, unreasoning force that had driven Will and my dash across America.

The hot crowded train packed with regular commuters had not deterred me. I crammed my body into the mass of office-dwelling flesh. The subway stank of perfume, aftershave, and deodorant and me, the last human smelling person on earth.

Deciding to enjoy the relatively fresh air of the city, I got off in the twenties and started walking south. I was still well north of the Trade Center when the first plane hit. I could hear the sound, like the sound of a major car crash but without the squeal of brakes. At least that is how I remember it. Of course, at the moment, I had no idea what the sound meant. I just figured that I was about to get a story. Deep inside I was still hoping that even if there was never to be a Pulitzer, I could get discovered, get a job on a real newspaper.

I pulled a camera from my jacket pocket, not my good one, one of those throwaways I carried around just in case, and started to jog toward the sound.

I had to weave through other pedestrians. Good New Yorkers, most of them were still going about their business. Crashes were too common to distract them. Later that September eleventh their lives would be totally affected. For that moment, they were, as they had been every other day, caught in their own individual frenzied worlds.

I pushed and ran as far as I could before pulling up against a building. Winded in the agony of the out-of-condition smoker, I leaned, breathless and frustrated, against a coarse brick doorway wedged between a bar and a cell phone store. I leaned and panted. Without thought, I stuck a cigarette in my mouth and lit it.

Two drags and then squashing the butt under my foot, I—half walking, half jogging and breathing hard—headed toward lower Manhattan. By the time I reached Houston Street, people were streaming northward, away from danger. Others were moving with equal determination toward the Trade Center, toward the noise.

The cacophony of sirens, people, and horns, played against my ears. The smells of fire and explosion. I kept moving, driven by some primordial determination, not for safety nor to help, but to see. Whatever had happened was big. I wanted to be there. I got a glimpse as the second plane crashed. I saw that moment with terror. I saw the flames and the smoke.

Streams of people had become torrents. One woman ran by in an evening dress, practically a ball gown, one of her heels broken. Lopsided as she ran, but run she did. I looked after her for a moment and thought of taking her picture.

She might be a good shot, maybe a great one.

Too late, she was gone.

A cry. I turned around and saw the first building crumble, the dust rising in a plume of destruction.

Again I moved forward, against the human tide, toward the devastation. I moved as if I were in a dream. Everything seemed at once unreal and fantastic and at the same moment so actual and so horribly concrete.

Sirens and horns and more sirens ripped through the morning, tearing at the horror, trying to reassure, to create order. There was no order, there was only the chaos of tragedy. People screamed at one another. Yet, there were no voices. Mouths opened and closed in grotesque mime.

The wrecking balls banging at the buildings of Alphabet City had been supplanted by the winged wrecking balls of unknown madness and vengeance banking at the heart of the city.

I choked on dust and sweated, perhaps from the heat of fires, perhaps from exertion, or perhaps from being so close to hell. My body shook. I wanted to scream, to cry, to pound my fist into something, someone. Teetering on the verge of madness.

I stopped knowing why I was pressing forward, where I was going, or what I might do. Action took the place of reason.

Abruptly, I stopped, caught by a sudden realization.

How the hell did Mo know? He knew. He tried to warn me.

I slumped against a plate-glass window. Behind it were fancy shoes and expensive bags. I was struck by how jumbled life is. Horrifying devastation next to luxurious indulgences.

Is Dad okay?

Who did this? Who was that Arab guy? Why was Mo following his sister? What the hell did Mo know, anyway?

Should I call Dad?

What the hell do I have to do with this? Did Jose's death …

My thoughts went in circles and circles within circles. I knew something terribly important, something terribly dangerous. That much Mo had made clear. I didn't know what it was, and I wasn't sure I wanted to know. Of one thing I was sure, I was in great danger, greater danger than I had been in right after Jose's murder. I heard Mo's voice, insistent in my head, telling me to get away, to get out of New York.

Get the hell out. Get out of New York. Far. Some small town far from here. Now. Don't wait.

I gasped for air, and I was grasping for truth.

"Hey, buddy, you all right?" A stranger was shaking me. "Buddy," he repeated, "do you need help?"

I stared at him. His face had seen a ghost, thousands of ghosts. Horror oozed from his pores. Nevertheless, he had stopped to help, to help me, a stranger.

"No, no, thanks," I whispered hoarsely. "I was thinking about a friend."

"Christ, there are going to be so many dead. Did your friend work in one of the towers?"

"No, not exactly."

"At a meeting, huh?"

I figured he needed to know something, some little detail about somebody, one little detail to hang on to, to make sense from. "Yeah, a meeting," I lied.

"Jesus, I hope he made it out okay."

"Me, too." That I wasn't lying about. I didn't know what had happened to Mo. I hoped he got out of town the way he had planned. Like the Good Samaritan who was still holding my arm and still looking intently into my face, I wanted something to clutch hold of—the drowning man grabbing at a straw. Somehow knowing Mo was all right would mean that I, too, would be all right.

I pulled my arm free from the man's grasp. His hand fell away. Confused, unsure if I should walk away, say something more, or hit him in the face and release my own tension.

"I hope you find him."

"Yeah, thanks." Not knowing if he heard me, but glad to have my irresolution over, I started to walk away.

"Good luck," he called still not willing to let go of that little corner of sanity our conversation had provided.

I can't find Mo, but I can look for Dad.

Without looking back, I waved in recognition and walked on, heading south, on towards the financial district.

Chapter 39: Dealing With Horror

I watched people jumping out of windows. I watched people burning to death. I watched people running in terror, and I watched others behaving heroically.

Was I a reporter or simply a voyeur?

Was I looking for my father or simply looking?

Did it matter?

I watched the chaos that life had become, and I wanted desperately to vomit, to purge myself of the sense of evil. And, I wanted to find oblivion, to get so stinking drunk that I could no longer think, that I didn't have to think.

The police tried to establish some semblance of order. I was told to move back north, back beyond Houston Street. Numbly, obediently, I stumbled up Broadway. A character out of Brecht: Mother Courage making her mind-numbed march of survival through the Hundred Years' War.

Sometimes, when we are at an end, when we are just surviving for the sake of survival, when we are marching blindly, mind-numbed through history, strange forces take over. In my case, the force was Sue, that wonderfully floppy-assed lime-green eyed avatar of forgetfulness and abandon.

There she was in front of me. Where she had come from I had no idea. What trick the fates were playing I had no knowledge. In the midst of madness the hedonism of animal lust and the escapism of meaningless sex took control. I let it happen.

While New York seethed with its cataclysm, while America held its collective breath, while the world stared at itself with the startled fear of a doe caught in the headlights, Sue and I checked into one of the ultimate fleabag hotels that abound in a metropolis. We fucked, screwed, and even made love.

The Gideons hadn't ignored even that rat hole. Next to the bed was one of the cheapest nightstands I'd ever seen. On its top lay a *Bible*. Just what a guy needs when he's with a whore. Sue was pissing, so I leafed through Biblical pages.

How the hell did Jesus meet his sexual needs? That last night, when he was in the garden, how did he deal with the tension if not screwing, jerking off?

Sue came out of the john and jumped on top of me. We were hard at it before I could put the *Bible* back. It fell to the floor with a small thud. "What the hell was that?" she asked.

"The word of God."

"Hey, you ain't one of those *holy rollers?*"

"Not so you'd notice."

"That's good. I don't like hypocrites."

"Neither do I."

That was the last thing I could say. She had reversed her position so that we could go for sixty-nine. I had my tongue buried in her sex. I could feel her expert tongue teasing me into renewal. My body shook with convulsions of pleasure. I moaned in forgetful contentment.

With nimbleness that belied her zaftig form, Sue vaulted off the bed. "I'd better get back to work. There'll be lots of escapist sex to sell today."

"Is that all this meant to you?"

She laughed. "Well, look who's talking."

I smiled weakly. "You have me there."

"There's nothing wrong with using sex to escape."

Sue picked up the *Bible* and tossed it onto the bed. The book flipped open to *Revelations*. I glanced down and shuddered at the thought of the end of the world. I couldn't help wondering if I had seen the first act that morning.

I thought of Mo's warning.

"I think I should get out of town."

"Oh?"

I was surprised, her tone actually suggested real interest.

"A friend kind of warned me. He thought I should get out of here, get far away."

"And, where is he?"

"Gone. At least I think ... no, I hope so. I hope he got out of town."

"Oh?" Again that tone.

"He said goodbye yesterday."

"Oh?"

I lay there holding the holy book and looking at Sue as she dressed. I got up, went to my clothes, and fished for my wallet. "How much?"

"Same as Baltimore."

I gave her sixty, then I pulled out an extra ten.

"Right."

I had an impulse, sudden, crazy and somehow absolutely right. "How about you? Want to come with me?"

"What are you talking about?"

"I told you, leaving town. This is not going to be a good place to live, at least not for a long time, not for me. I was thinking of going out West somewhere. Starting over. You want to come?"

"Why would you want the company of a used-up, exotic dancer whore?" Sue looked at the ceiling, then turned to face me. Her eyes flashed with anger. "Hey, you don't think that I'm gonna support you? It ain't gonna happen."

"No. Honest. That was not what I was thinking."

"I don't know why the hell Mo cared," she bit off the last word.

"What did you say?" I demanded.

"I said I didn't know why you cared."

"The hell you did. You know Mo. You worked for him. You worked for him?"

"Who the hell is Mo?" She rolled her eyes to indicate incredulity. It didn't work. In bed Sue was a great actor. Out of it, she was strictly no-talent. Her eye-roll was straight from vaudeville, overly done and not convincing.

"No good, Sue … if your name is Sue?"

"What the hell are you talking about?"

"Your connection to the *Mossad*, to my buddy Mo, to following me around."

She tried again. "You're nuts. I think I'll call you Mr. Planters."

"Call me whatever you want, but tell me the truth." She moved toward the door, but I got there first and was standing with my back to it. She probably could have outwrestled me. Instead, with a sigh, she gave in.

"Yeah. Mo. Yeah, I know him."

Chapter 40: Flights

The trip from Oregon back to New York had been anticlimactic.

Will and I had accomplished nothing except a helter-skelter race propelled by unknown forces. Not a decent apple pie or an experience to tell about.

After a couple of days of hanging out with a bottle and a joint, it was time for me to head back to The Big Apple. My buddy took me to the airport and watched, with a clear sense of relief, as I wobbled down the walkway to the plane. By the time I reached Chicago, where I had to change planes, I was hung over. I decided to smoke a bowl to settle my stomach.

Shit, that was bad weed. It worked just the opposite. I puked my guts out. It was the last time I did weed. Sadly, it was not the last time I'd get heaving drunk.

So that was my image of the vast American continent, a race interspersed with drunken puke, a real invitation.

It didn't matter. What did matter was escaping from the madness, the anger and paranoia that were sweeping over New York and the personal paranoia that was creeping over me. Sue had been the last straw.

She wouldn't, or perhaps couldn't, tell me why it was so important to Mo that she watch over me and keep me sexually satisfied. Maybe she knew no more than I. She did know Mo had used a miniature homing device sewn into a seam in my favorite military knock-off jacket, the one I almost always wore no matter what else was under or on top. I bought that jacket at a flea market when I was still in high school and I loved it, loved it all the more because it offended my father, as anti-military a guy as one would ever meet. Like all good adolescents I was dependent on him and resented the fact. A symbol of rebellion was called for. Looking back, it might have been better if I had rebelled all the way and joined up.

How complicated family loyalties become. I revered my father. I still do. I put him on a pedestal and then wanted … want … to pull him down. I rage at my deranged mother and still can't let her go. I keep going back to that well to taste the water only to find that it's as poisoned as it always was. Even my brother. I keep hoping for Jim's redemption. I know it will never come, but pray I must.

As I always do when life becomes overwhelming for me, I turned to the old man. At least he was safe. Only time would tell the effects of the ash that rained down on Lower Manhattan that day, but for now he was safe. Ironically, in the midst of the devastation wrought by the hijackers, his garage was prospering. Workers needed parking. Always the Boy Scout, Dad cut the rates, but the demand for parking was, for the moment, twenty-four seven.

I guess Dad has never given up on me. He has encouraged and paved the way with his money. I suppose he did some praying, too. We've never discussed those intimate details. We never did when I was a kid, so why should we change now? Hopes, fears, faith, loves, desires, those were too personal to share as father and son. How sad. How human. How quintessentially American.

Once again I turned to him. Once again Dad came through. His newest girlfriend, yeah, of course he was cheating on Sylvia, had a car she wanted to get rid of, an old black Ford, not anything I'd normally want to buy, but dependable with less than sixty thousand on the odometer. Dad gave me the old Ford and eight hundred in cash and promised more if I needed.

I was ready to run. Where? That was still the question. I figured I'd leave it to fate. I'd travel into the hinterlands and stop when I found a job.

The second question was did I still want Sue to come with me? If I did, would she want to come? Perhaps she still felt responsible for me. If that was to be her reason for joining my flight, I wanted no part of it. If Mo was still pulling strings to protect me, I wanted free of that, too. I wanted Sue with me as I had thought of her before she had fessed-up, as the sweet fat-assed hooker who seemed to turn up when I needed her. I wanted her voluptuous sexuality, her willingness, her surprising physicality, the dexterity of her orifices, and the security blanket of her presence.

When does want turn to desire? Does desire somehow turn into love?

Before she left the hotel room on September eleventh, Sue gave me her pager number. Over the next couple of days, I called five times.

Finally, when I was ready to give up and terrified that I would have to, she called back.

We met in Central Park. It seemed a fitting place to discuss going into Middle America. We talked for an hour. Walked for another.

We found a little restaurant and bought coffee and Danish. We sat and talked for another hour.

The waiter asked if we wanted anything else. Not wanting the conversation to end, I ordered another Danish, cheese.

The waiter clunked the plate down with a nasty frown. I picked the pastry up. "I wonder if there will be decent Danish."

"Where?"

"Wherever I end up."

Before I could take a bite, Sue reached over took the Danish from my hand and bit into it.

"Good?"

"Yeah." She held it suspended as if she were studying a work of genius. "Probably not." She put the pastry back on the chipped off-white plate. "It won't be New York. Probably no pastrami either."

"No."

I picked up the pastry and took a bite. "Not bad."

Her face grew serious. "I guess I'll go with you."

"You will? For real?" Suddenly, I knew how much I needed her. I wanted her sexually, but I also wanted her as part of my life. "Great. When can we leave?"

"Tomorrow. Today. I'm ready. Whenever."

"Are you sure?"

"No. I just think it's the right thing to do."

"Why?" Suddenly I was suspicious.

"You really want to know?"

"Yeah."

"Because you didn't object to my taking a bite of your lousy Danish."

"What?"

"You know where my mouth has been. You know what it's done. Hell, you know that better than almost anyone." She laughed a little, then turned steely-eyed serious. "You don't judge me. You're not repulsed by it. Who the hell better to be with?"

"Who the hell," I echoed.

We had crossed The George by eight that evening. Taking turns, we drove through the night. At daybreak we stopped at a rat-hole motel in Indiana.

We bought some Einstein bagels and coffee at a nearby shopping center. "These taste like the Midwest," I said as we lay on the lumpy bed and ate breakfast.

Sue laughed and slurped her coffee. She took it with lots of sugar and half-and-half.

"What's so funny?"

"Us. The two New York sophisticates."

"Running for my life."

"That part isn't so funny."

"But why?"

"Why what?"

"Why would anyone want to kill me?"

"Obviously because of what you know."

I took a long slug of coffee and wished that it were booze. "That's just it. I don't know what I know. Nobody cares about Jose Figurés. Even if they did, that story went down in flames with the World Trade Center. Nobody is going to do anything in downtown Manhattan, not now. Certainly nothing in Alphabet City. It's over ... isn't it?"

"What's the connection?" Sue asked taking another bite of the roll that was masquerading as a bagel.

"What connection?"

"Between Jose and the attack?"

"None. He was dead. Besides—" I had no idea what we were talking about.

"There has to be something. What? Who?"

"I have no idea. Honestly. Maybe Mo—"

"He never said anything to you?" she asked.

"Just that I was better off not knowing what I knew."

We drank more coffee and lit cigarettes.

"What about you?" I asked.

She shook her head. "He never told me anything. Why would he? My job was just to make sure you were okay."

"He worried about me?"

"Yeah, he did." Sue kissed me gently. "I think he really cared about you … sort of like a kid brother."

I shrugged. "Yeah, sure."

Funny, there were times I wished he were my brother, the big brother I'd always wanted.

"You went to Washington," Sue said in a subdued voice. "What did you …? Why did you go? It must have been important. Mo …"

She stopped. I searched her face and found no answers.

It hit me. "The pictures. The god-damned pictures." I almost yelled it. With the thought came a resurgence of fear.

I sat, my back against the propped up pillows and stared into Sue's eyes. I wanted to softly sink into those lime green pools of Sue's love. I wanted to find safety, to run away from the thoughts that were burning inside.

Love? Did Mo love me? Do I love Sue? Is that possible?

Still, I couldn't shake the images of that snowy afternoon. I saw Burmaste. I saw the Arab.

Holy shit! John Hunter, the invisible bastard. Whoever he is. Whatever he does. He may not exist, but he's the nexus.

The realization terrified me. Somehow, somewhere, deep within the U.S. government there was a connection named, at least in my mind, in my life, named John Hunter. It was a connection with evil.

I said nothing to Sue. It was my secret, one I planned to keep unspoken for the rest of my life. One thing was sure, if I said the words, I'd be in danger.

The hell with me. I would be putting Sue in danger, too.

Chapter 41: A Great Responsibility

We wouldn't have survived the years since if it hadn't been for Sue. She works a grocery store cash register and cuts pennies wherever she can.

And, my old man has been good for a few bucks here and there.

Of course, I work. I got another reporting job on another going-nowhere weekly. The only difference is, besides school lunches and Little League, now I write about crops, weather trends, and the prices of commodities. I interview farmers, John Deere salesmen, even crop dusters. No Pulitzers here.

We get by.

But, man does not live by bread alone. Loneliness and horniness are two major curses. I would wish someone dead before those twin demons take over his life, and having seen the massacre that day, I don't wish people dead very easily. Sue has been my company and my sexual companion. I am truly grateful for both.

We set up housekeeping in a small apartment on the outskirts of town. We even went down to the pound and got ourselves a dog, a Pomeranian-Spitz mix, ugly, but loving. That was the important thing, loving. We named her Shirley.

Sue wanted me to forget the whole thing, the entire story of Mo, Jose, The World Trade Center, the trip to the Washington suburbs, and the unlikely people I'd seen there. She wanted me to stop worrying at the questions I couldn't articulate and the answer I refused to discuss. I tried to take her advice. I buried the entire subject in the dead-letter section of my brain.

I would have continued to live that way except for the plane crash.

I hadn't noticed it on the ticker right off. I was busy covering local shit, too busy for the national news. It was an election year and it seemed like everyone in town wanted to be mayor, or alderman, or some kind of elected official with access to the public trough. Personally, I didn't think any of them were good enough to be crossing guards, let alone dogcatchers. Then, I still had that big-city mind.

A few months after the election, a small plane crashed, nothing big just some unimportant local flight. I was trying to do a piece about small planes and their safety record. It had been the editor's idea, something to reassure people that our local air service with its puddle jumpers wasn't dangerous.

So, I was going through stories about small plane crashes. Just reading a few lines and looking at the pictures, just getting ideas, just looking for inspiration. Photographs do that for me, give me ideas about how to write, what point of view to take.

Oh my God, that's him. … And him.

The man I knew as John Hunter: tall, thin, owl eyes, thick glasses. The man who had so strangely connected the various threads of Alphabet City. Not identified in the picture, but I recognized him instantly. Grabbing a magnifying glass I assured myself.

And standing slightly behind him, somebody even more terrifying, the drunk from the train. Not wearing a green suit, but definitely the same guy.

They knew each other. He was on that train because of me. What was he supposed to do?

I dug out the Xeroxes I had made before I gave Mo the pictures.

Yeah, the same guys.

The photograph had been taken in Minnesota. It had been right before Paul Wellstone's plane had taken off, shortly before it had crashed killing the respected senator, his wife and daughter. John Hunter and the guy from the train had been there just before the death of this major liberal politician, the man whom some were already touting as a potential president.

The picture hit like a ton of bricks. No way to handle it. There had to be something wrong. They weren't there by chance, standing in the background trying to look inconspicuous.

"How much money was involved?" I asked myself. "What the hell were they after?"

"What are you talking about?" Jen, who worked the next desk, asked. I hadn't realized I was talking aloud.

"Sorry. Nothing important. Just talking to myself."

"Crazy or money?"

"What?"

"Talking to yourself. Are you crazy or do you have money in the bank?"

"On our salaries, it can't be money."

Jen laughed. I had expected her to. It gave me a chance to end the conversation and pick up the phone.

I called Sue.

We met back at our apartment.

I had to share it with her.

I explained the connection in my mind, the one between Hunter, the CIA, the mob, the Arabs and money, money that evil men had thought would buy off other evil men. For the mob, for the Arabs, the money had been the big thing. But for the others, for the shadowy figures, the people who made up and controlled the guy I knew as Hunter, for the Burmastes of the world, it was about power, the power that money would buy, the power to control American politics, the power to steer the great ship.

"They were all in it together," I told Sue. "They were all taking their piece of the action; just one big happy scam. Mob, CIA, Arabs, the damned city government, all one greedy family. And to think that good old Jose, an idealist, a community organizer, got in their way. If he had just allowed himself to be bought off, if they made all the money they were after, would the Arabs still have taken out the Towers? Did they hate us that much?"

I already knew the answer. I had learned it in Peru. Yes, a lot of the world did hate us that much. I had figured it out. Here at home there were plenty who viewed the rest of us with that much contempt.

We talked and we cried. We cried for the thousands of dead, for Jose, for the hapless people of Alphabet City who had lost their homes, for the hapless people who had been conned into buying those unstable buildings, and for those who had been dispossessed from their Alphabet City hovels to make room for the sales pitch of progress.

We cried. When we had cried enough, I got angry. "I want to kill that bastard."

"Which one?"

"All of them. Hunter."

"He's just a tool."

"I know that. Not even his name. But, he deserves to die. They think they can steal this country."

"And that other guy, was he supposed to kill me? To make sure there were no photographs?" I shook with fear.

We sat on the couch. Sue held me. We rocked in each other's arms while Shirley jumped on us and tried to lick our faces.

We laughed. Her antics? Our anxiety?

Joined by the horror of what I finally understood and the comfort of our togetherness, Sue and I made love. We lay together on our secondhand couch with its absurd upholstery: a bear attacking, salmon leaping up a river to spawn, deer in the background merged into a jigsaw jumble of trees—the wilderness of old captured in our twelve-by-nine living room.

We made love, and the dog tried to lick our toes. When we finished, we talked some more, stupid stuff like groceries, work, and neighbors. We desperately wanted our world to again seem normal.

We went into the yard and played with Shirley. I'd throw a stick and she'd bark wildly while Sue encouraged her. Then I'd jog across the grass, get the stick, and do it again.

We sat on the ground. Absently, I scratched the dog's ears and Sue rubbed my back. Then Sue held Shirley's hulking body on her lap as I kneaded her shoulders.

I went inside, to the cabinet to get Shirley's food. Sue followed. For a second time that day we made love, me leaning against the counter, Sue sitting on my hips, her legs clasped around me. Shirley, ever-impatient dog, whimpered in anticipation and scratched at my legs.

"I love you," I said.

"Me, too."

Finally, we went to bed.

In the middle of the night I woke up. Awakened by music, the angelic floating music of a pan flute. Closing my eyes I was back in Peru, back at the place where time is held forever. I listened to the music. It was the voices of the gods.

"It is a great responsibility to have heard the voice of God." That had been Mo's comment at Machu Picchu. Finally, I understood what he meant. I had been made a witness.

There is no responsibility greater than bearing witness.

The thought terrified me.

Quietly, so as to not disturb Sue, I got up.

I went into the living room, Shirley padding after.

My teeth were clenched and my jaw hurt. I got my old word processor out of the closet, put it on the coffee table, and started writing.

I may be the last person who uses a word processor, but I prefer it to computers. Computers are for the office. I guess my real objection to them is that you never know who might creep into your home though the Internet. A little paranoid? I just do not want anyone tapping into my ideas before they are all in place.

I want to put the story on paper, everything I know as honestly as I can. I'm not even sure I want this story published, but I need to write it, to tell the tale, to clear my mind, to try and get perspective. I need to be the witness that the gods intended.

I know Sue will approve. What about Estrella? What would she think? Ah, she'll probably never know. Still.

Finally, I had my story, not a Pulitzer story but a truth.

It is the story that counts, not the fame, not the prize. Am I doing it justice?

The yellow of dawn is crawling across the rug.

Damn, I need sleep. Sleep, or coffee, or both.

***

There are song lyrics circling my brain, a song I learned years ago.

It was Easter vacation. Reluctantly, Dad had agreed, Jim and I could go to Florida. Mom and Paul met us in Miami. She hugged and kissed us and tried to make us hug Paul. Tall, thin, with a neat beard and almost bald, he suggested shaking hands instead.

Paul drove a battered pickup. Jim and I sat with our backs against the cab and talked as we swept onto the keys and down the Overseas Highway.

We stopped in Marathon for burgers and key lime pie. Mom beamed as she talked excitedly about the three men in her life. Paul held her hand and chorused, "That's right," to everything she said.

"She seems really happy," I said when we were back in the truck.

"Yeah, sure," Jim answered.

Jim and I slept on the floor of the main cabin. Paul's houseboat had only the one bedroom where he and Mom slept. To get to the bathroom, Jim and I had to go through that bedroom, which made things very uncomfortable. Even worse, we could hear them during the night. Jim vented his anger on my arms, which were soon black-and-blue. I vented mine in phone calls to Dad, who promised me a new bike when we got home.

There were a few other kids visiting from up North. During the days, we swam in the marina, ignoring the slick of diesel fuel, and hiked around town.

Every evening Mom, Paul, Jim, and I watched the sun go down on the Gulf side of town. Paul would talk about Hemingway and how he loved to fish, to watch the sunset, and to drink. Paul loved to drink, too. Mostly he drank beer, but he drank lots of it.

Our last night in Key West there was a campfire on Smathers Beach. A bunch of the folks from the marina were there. There were hotdogs and Cokes. We kids played tag and wiffle ball and the grownups joined in. A few people had guitars, so they played and sometimes we all sang.

We sat on blankets and watched the fire. The wood crackled, and sparks flew upwards.

"They are like shooting stars, Mom said.

"What does that mean?"

"You can make a wish on them and your wish will come true."

I wanted to wish something wonderful. I wanted to wish that we could be happy. That Mom and Dad were back together. That Jim was not so mean to me. That life would be different. That happy could be forever.

That was what I wanted to wish, but I didn't. I knew better. I knew that good times would always go away the same way that Mom kept leaving. For any happiness of that night, I remember more its sadness, the sadness of inevitable endings. And I remember one of the songs we sang sitting around that campfire and watching the sparks carry our wishes to the heavens.

"These are the times,
The terrible times,
The times to try the soul of man.
These are the terrible times."

86

Author's Afterward

Some of this story is based on fact and some is pure fiction. The strange thing is that much which reads like fiction, is actually fact. The events told in this book are based on the experience of a dear friend, one of the people mentioned in the dedication. There was a murder. There was an attempt to develop Alphabet City even though there was no bedrock beneath. There was a trip to Machu Picchu. There was a Mossad connection. And, of course, there was 9/11, a day that will haunt us forever. Based on that framework, I created this tale. I emphasize that it is a novel, not a work of history.

A few people deserve thanks for their help with this book. Thanks to my editor Jacob Shaver as well as to my wife for her editorial assistance. Thanks to All Things That Matter Press for its continuing support of my writing.

Writing the prologue of *Times to Try the Soul of Man* was particularly difficult. Nick had to be slimy enough to elicit reactions, but he also had to offer enough sense of potential redemption to get readers involved. I thank the various people who over the years have read that chapter and helped me to refine it.

In the end, Nick not only finds redemption, but who also bears witness to something important: There are many who would take over our world, who would happily subvert us as individuals and as a society for their ends. It is the responsibility of each of us to speak out against that subversion. We may not be part of the Fourth Estate, but we all have that responsibility.

Kenneth Weene
February, 2015

About the Author

Kenneth Weene is a peaceful man, a psychologist and author by inclination. However, when confronted by the evils of this world, he arms himself with the best weapon at his disposal, the written word.

Ken is also author of *Widow's Walk* and *Memoirs From the Asylum*, both published by All Things That Matter Press.

www.ingramcontent.com/pod-product-compliance
Lightning Source LLC
Chambersburg PA
CBHW051646260626
47170CB00004B/1367